For Bruce, Jim, and Dean.

Their devotion, sweet nature and sharp
intelligence inspired, and continue to inspire,
the sheepdog character, Sidney.

CHAPTER 1

A Crush Party In Wine Country

"Wow—what a beauty! Few collectors of my stature own such a valuable treasure. I must have it!"

Lucy and Tim Newman's friends were happily milling about inside the Newman's wine cellar on a crisp autumn night while waiting for the grapes to arrive for Crush.

They sampled prior vintages of Tim's wine label *L'homme Nouveau* served by Peter Smith, a blond man dressed in blue designer jeans and red Keniworth Winery parka. They also tasted delicious hors d'oeuvres being passed around by silver-haired Bob Goodwin, owner of the Sonoma catering company Not Just Olives.

"Wow...this Zin's *delicious*," Tom White swirled the rich ruby colored wine in his glass.

"*Agreed*," Peter Smith replied, smiling. "Tim's wine is the same quality as our Keniworth wines. Of course, it always helps to have access to top quality grapes *and* the occasional assistance of a world class winemaker," Peter added, raising his eyebrow at a man with boyish good looks.

Tim grinned back. "You're correct, Peter." Tim turned to face his friends. "Full disclosure, everyone. The Bartino Family, one of the best growers in Sonoma County, provides our excellent grapes. Peter's boss, Jeremy Keniworth, advises us when to harvest our grapes and how to make our wines. A few years ago, Jeremy warned us to harvest just before a freak late summer storm caused bunch rot in many vineyards."

"If our engagement wine contains this much radical truth, it'll be awesome," gushed Harold Brewster, an entrepreneur-in-residence at a biotech venture capital firm. "Attending Crush is truly mindful," he added stroking his long dark rectangular beard. "Deidre and I can't thank you enough for giving us ten cases of this year's vintage as an engagement present."

"Harold, as an early stage investor in your awesome start-up, it's the least I can do," Tim replied smiling. "I probably owe you a million cases. Here's to your engagement to Deidre. Congratulations!" The group clinked their glasses.

"Tim, I'd like to know more about your private label wine," the narrow-faced, grey-haired venture capitalist Marc Todd moved his nose closer to his wine glass. "Why did you decide put your cellar *here*?" He asked in the quiet low-key voice accustomed to assessing young start-ups for his Sand Hill Road venture firm.

"That's so like a VC," Tim teased. "Always scouting out the business model behind every project—even a hobby winery like this."

The group chuckled as Tim signaled them to accompany him outside.

"Our wine cellar is in a shaded area close to a creek. These ancient oak and willow trees provide a natural canopy that keeps the wine cool as it ages in the barrel," Tim pointed to nearby trees. "After Lucy and I built the wine cellar and purchased our winemaking equipment, we discovered that we can produce 100 cases a year of fine quality wine at very low cost in this modest cellar.

"To answer Marc's question, our business model is simple. It's based on cheap capital—our own—and even cheaper labor from us and our friends. We've assembled a team of Silicon Valley folk who want to learn about winemaking without the cost and hassle of owning a winery or vineyard. We reward our friends with wine. Our bottling parties in the spring are loads of fun. You'll be invited to our next bottling party, as long as you're willing to work for wine."

"You'd better watch out for Sonoma creek wildlife. A woodrat might eat its way into your wine barrels and drink the wine," Tom White joked in a gravelly voice reminiscent of his service with the U.S. Marines.

"Stop it, Tom," his wife Leslie quipped. "You'll spook people." Looking up at the willow trees, she continued. "Our Sonoma creeks are rich with wildlife, including red-shouldered hawks, elegant green herons, white-breasted songbirds, sparrow like towhees, and the enterprising but cute dusky-footed woodrat."

"True," Tom barked as everyone smiled.

"How can a rat ever be cute or enterprising?" Marc Todd frowned skeptically.

"Don't be put off by the name," Leslie cautioned. "A woodrat is a buff colored little creature with cute Mickey Mouse ears that's more akin to a gerbil. It grooms itself like a cat and lives for many generations in the same elaborate wood-nest made from twigs, branches, and other items scavenged from creeks. It lines its nest with herbs to keep out pests. Naturalists get very excited if they spot one because they rarely venture out before dark."

"Leslie's correct," Tom added. "We recently learned more about our fascinating local animals and birds after joining a wildlife preservation group. Now that we're better informed, we've observed the magnificent red-shouldered hawk flying around Sonoma and highways 121 and 37 close to the Bay."

"I noticed several fierce-looking hawks hovering or perched by 121 when I drove up here," Marc replied. "I felt as if I was under surveillance." The group chuckled.

"I recently spotted an elegant white heron near Schellville," serial entrepreneur Jason Lee noted, his eyes shining with enthusiasm. "I see beautiful creatures all the time when I ride the Sand Hill Portola Valley bicycle loop. However, I haven't seen a white heron in this area until recently, even though I've owned a second home up here for years."

Leslie nodded, smiling. "Jason, you're very observant. Recently, our local wildlife group reported that many new birds and bird species are arriving and nesting here. We think it's the result of the new wetland restoration projects close by. When they converted the old decommissioned Hamilton Air Force Base into a fish and wildlife refuge, they breached a levee to allow the Bay to enter the area for the first time in more than 100 years. During the last decade they've also planted native grasses and shrubs to help restore valuable former wetlands."

"Wow, I'm impressed," Tim raised his eyebrows as he looked at Tom and Leslie. "I need to pay more attention." The rest of the group nodded in agreement with Tim.

Several guests weren't listening. They were inside the wine cellar admiring Deidre Langton's magnificent engagement ring, a large pink diamond surrounded by a circle of white diamonds. Deidre, Harold's fiancée, extended her lovely hand for admirers.

"Darling, we've seen some exquisite jewelry in our time, haven't we?" purred Lady Roberta Romakoff, a tall, slim, brunette to her friend, former British supermodel-turned-vintner, Amanda Jones. "Even during my days with Dmitri, I never saw a diamond *this* gorgeous."

"*Crikey,*" Amanda replied in a rich, husky British voice. Her long, wavy silver hair draped over Deidre's arm as she leaned over to gaze at the ring. "This diamond looks as if it belongs with the Crown Jewels in the Tower of London. It must have cost a *bloody fortune.*"

"The setting reminds me of Princess Diana's engagement ring," muttered Realtor Samantha Pond as she shook her head. "I have to admit, ladies, I'm turning green with envy."

Amanda gave a throaty laugh. "Aren't we all, darling?"

"This ring has a romantic history," Deidre, a petite brunette explained as she allowed the women in the group to stare longingly at her left hand. "It was once owned by a mistress of King Louis XIV of France. This mistress was nicknamed *La Violette* because she wore magnificent violet and purple gowns around Versailles.

"Rumor has it that the ring was smuggled out of France during the French Revolution. After that, the ring passed from owner to owner—

sometimes by sale, sometimes by theft—provoking awe, outrage, and the occasional murder. When it finally turned up in a valuable antiques auction in London, Harold made a special trip to bid for this ring. My history students are dazzled by it," she smiled.

"Deidre, it's a stunner…but you'll have to take it off when we start crushing grapes," Amanda cautioned. "When the grapes arrive, all of us take turns throwing grapes into the crusher and you definitely wouldn't want your ring ending up in there, too."

"Good thinking," advised Lady Roberta. "You wouldn't want that gorgeous ring accidently mangled and crushed like a grape, would you?"

"Would you like me to lock it away in our bedroom safe?" Lucy, a slim blonde woman felt she should offer as the vintner host.

Deidre looked at the beautiful jewels on her left hand and sighed. "Lucy, I don't want to put you to any trouble. Don't worry, ladies. I'll keep it safe when we start crushing the grapes."

As the other guests helped themselves to more wine and hors d'oeuvres, Deidre looked around the cellar and noticed several handsome wooden barrels stacked against the back wall. She went to the wine barrels and surreptitiously took off her ring. She bent down and placed it on a wooden ledge behind one of the wine racks. *"There,"* she thought to herself, *"Now I can enjoy Crush without worrying about this darn ring. I wish Harold's rich friends would show an interest in something other than my engagement ring."*

The guests heard the roar of shifting gears as a large agricultural truck came up the driveway. They went outside to watch Charlie Bartino expertly turn his truck and reverse it toward the front entrance of the cellar, revealing three large bulk bin containers filled with grapes.

While Charlie parked, Tim ran into the cellar and returned driving a forklift. He stood up with one hand on the wheel and addressed the group.

"Hi everyone, here's the plan. That machine over there in the center of our cellar is known as a crusher or de-stemmer. I need a couple of guys to help us maneuver Charlie's bulk bins onto this forklift. After I drive the forklift to the crusher, I'll need a couple more guys to help me position the bins. After we get the bins in place, we'll scoop the grapes into the crusher. After this machine removes the stems and crushes the grapes, juice will flow from the bottom into a vat. Once we've crushed the grapes tonight, I'll add yeast to the vat tomorrow to start the fermentation process."

"This is the fun part," said Amanda Jones to her women friends. "We ladies get to ruin our manicures by stuffing grapes into the crusher. However, I wouldn't miss this for the world. I love every minute of it."

"Ah-hah! Crush has started. They're all busy with the grapes. No one's watching me or the handsome sparkly hidden behind the wine barrels. With luck, I'll grab the jewel before anyone notices it's missing."

CHAPTER 2

Sidney Learns The Diamond Ring Is Missing

Tim and Lucy Newman's long-haired Australian Shepherd, Sidney was jolted awake when a vehicle with flashing lights and a loud radio pulled into the driveway.

"*Strewth!*" Sidney exclaimed in the dialect of his ancestors, who'd picked up the Australian accent from Australian sheep imported into the US in the 1800s. "*It's our local Sonoma County Sheriff's Department,*" he woofed.

Sidney pushed his nose against the windowpane. He observed two sheriff's deputies getting out of the police cruiser. Sidney was annoyed that he was shut inside the house. He couldn't boss and herd his humans during the Crush party in the wine cellar. He was also upset that the daughter of the house, Catherine, was away for a sleepover with friends, where he couldn't protect her. In between loud angry barks and yelps, he listened for clues about why the police had arrived at *his* home.

Tim came around the side to the front of the building. "Hi, I'm Tim Newman. Thank you for coming so promptly."

"Hi, Mr. Newman. I'm Deputy Ben Morris," the uniformed police officer said as he shook hands with Tim. "This is my partner, Deputy Dan Carter."

"Is that an Aussie I hear barking?" Deputy Dan Carter asked as he saw Sidney's pouting face peering from the window by the front door.

"Yes, it's our Aussie, Sidney. He's usually very sweet tempered but tonight he's upset about being stuck inside. We didn't want him injured by Charlie Bartino's truck delivering our grapes earlier this evening. We also didn't want sticky grape juice all over his long fur while we were crushing the grapes, either. Unreasonable … huh?"

The policemen smiled. "Aussies are smart dogs. Do you think they'd make good police dogs?" Officer Morris asked.

"Yes … if you let them run your entire department," joked Tim. "They're very bossy."

Sidney raced from room to room monitoring Tim and the deputies walking to the back of the property. Sidney stood by the French windows as Tim and the deputies entered a large brown barn-shaped building.

"Will someone please tell me what's going on," he howled. *"I can't leave my human herd alone for one split second without someone getting into a whole host of trouble,"* he protested in loud barks. *"It's hell herding humans. I'd be better off herding sheep."*

A dapper green heron flew close to an open side window and chirped loudly. *"Sidney, stop sulking like a spoiled Aussie. Tim called the police because Deidre's engagement ring has disappeared."*

Sidney stopped barking and looked up as the heron came to rest just outside the window. She was joined by a local white-breasted nuthatch songbird. *"From what we heard from the nearby trees, Harold —her fiancée—is mad as heck,"* chirped the heron. *"He insisted Tim call the police and report the theft before anyone left the premises."*

"Sounds like one of the humans has done something dumb—again," Sidney growled.

"Deidre and everyone in the wine cellar are very upset," sang the songbird sadly.

"That's terrible," whimpered Sidney, pacing up and down by the French windows. *"Harold's tech speak is baffling to me…but I love Deidre. She must be devastated. I wish someone would let me into the wine cellar. Humans, even the police, don't have an acute sense of smell."*

After several moments of quiet while Sidney tried to listen to what was happening in the wine cellar, he sighed with disgust. *"If they hadn't shut me inside, I could've stopped the thief from making off with the ring."*

"I doubt it," retorted the green heron. *"Most thieves are very devious."*

"Jays are the worst thieves," sang the nuthatch. *"They steal other birds' food! Even food from other blue jays."*

"Even if I didn't notice the thief steal the ring, I might be able to identify the culprit with my sensitive nose," replied Sidney with slightly haughty indignation. *"A retired police dog at the dog park told me that humans get very nervous when they commit crimes. They leave a sweaty scent. Smart sheepdogs like us can trace it. Trouble is…any sweaty scent may disappear by the time I can investigate."*

Sidney stared at the huge gates of the wine cellar waiting for more information. When the humans finally appeared, Lucy walked towards the house with her arm was around Deidre's shoulders. Deidre looked shocked. Harold scowled, walking beside Tim. The rest of the guests walked slowly, eyes on the ground, hands in pockets.

Lucy unlocked the French windows as everyone moved inside. Sidney rushed to comfort Deidre. After she sat on the couch, Sidney sat by her and leaned his large furry body against her legs.

"Sidney, don't bother Deidre," Tim chided. "Come here."

"Oh, please don't scold Sidney…he's *fine*," replied Deidre. She stroked Sidney's fur with affection. Pretending that he hadn't heard Tim's command, Sidney looked mournfully into her eyes.

Deputy Ben Morris informed the group that they'd like to interview everyone present. "Tim, do you have a study or another private area can use?"

"Shouldn't you be *searching* everyone to find my fiancée's diamond ring?" Harold asked sharply.

The room fell silent as the deputies calmly ignored Harold's outburst. They followed Tim out of the room and into his home office. Once inside the office, Dan Carter closed the door.

"Mr. Newman, with your cooperation, we'll keep the wine cellar locked up until our forensics team arrives. Is that OK with you?"

Tim nodded his head vigorously. "That's 100% OK with me," he replied. "I want this situation cleared up as quickly as possible."

"We'd also appreciate you allowing our forensics team to search the rest of the property," the deputy added. "If they're given complete access, they may be able to shed some light on what happened to this ring."

"Of course," Tim replied. "I'll do everything I can to help."

"We'd also like interview individually everyone present when the ring disappeared to see if they have any ideas. That may take some time. Is that OK with you? Can we use this office for the interviews?"

"Yes, absolutely. I'm sure they'll do their best to help," Tim replied.

After Tim and the deputies left the room, Deidre stood up to confront her fiancé.

"Harold, how *could* you be so mean as to accuse anyone here of stealing my ring? I still think it's fallen down somewhere in the dark. Maybe the police will find it but it's far too early to accuse anyone."

Harold's dark eyes flashed with anger. "Deidre, I'm only trying to find out what happened to the valuable ring that you *so stupidly* left on a wooden ledge behind some wine barrels."

The room fell silent. Charlie Bartino was the first to recover.

"Hey, that's no way to talk to the charming lady you're about to make your bride. Have a little respect. In my book, people are more important than baubles—however valuable."

"Darlings, I'm all for being searched if that will clear things up," said Amanda tossing her lovely head with indignation.

"Oh, I *so* agree," said Lady Roberta. "The police can *strip search* me anytime they want. Only happy to oblige," she said glaring at Harold.

"Me too," added Samantha.

"Stop it everyone," shouted Deidre with tears welling in her eyes. "I feel terrible about what happened! I know it's all my fault…but I can't stand listening to you bickering." She ran from the room. Lucy followed her, almost tripping over Sidney, who rushed to comfort and protect Deidre.

After a long pause Harold looked at Charlie. "Sir, you're right. I apologize. I'm sorry I lost it. I didn't mean to accuse anyone. I certainly didn't intend to insult Deidre. I feel like a total jerk." He ran his hand through his hair.

Tom White, a Silicon Valley COO, consoled his friend. "Don't worry, Harold. We all sympathize. You could have shown more tact but none of us have dealt with this type of situation before." He chuckled. "Come to think of it, it was little dumb of your lovely fiancée to leave her valuable ring on a ledge in the back of the wine cellar."

"Tom, smart people make dumb mistakes all the time in Silicon Valley," Leslie retorted. "Let's be kind to the lovely schoolteacher who's lost her engagement ring...and who's trying *not* to blame the rest of us."

"Was the ring insured?" Tom asked quietly.

"I suppose so," mumbled Harold. "God, I don't exactly know. I leave all that stuff to my insurance broker."

CHAPTER 3

Catherine And Sidney Comfort Deidre

The next morning, Lucy ascended the stairs to her guest house. "Deidre, can I have a word?"

Deidre and Harold were busy packing their suitcases. After Deidre learned that Harold had apologized for losing his temper, they had reconciled. However, neither had slept well. They couldn't wait to get back to the quiet privacy of their home in Palo Alto.

Deidre opened the door. "Of course, Lucy. What's up?"

"My daughter Catherine's returned from her sleepover . We told her about the ring being stolen last night. She wants to talk to you."

Deidre inwardly sighed. Harold quickly interposed. "Lucy that's really nice … but we need to get back to Palo Alto ASAP."

Seeing Lucy's anxious face, Deidre's patience and fondness for children came to the fore.

"Harold, let's see what Catherine wants. She's only a child. She might be unnerved by what's happened and need some reassurance."

"Deidre, you're so right," Harold said. "Come to that, I could do with a little reassurance myself."

Deidre laughed and gave Harold a hug. Lucy went outside to summon her daughter. Moments later, a child with long blonde hair marched up the steps to the guest house. Sidney raced up the steps behind her.

"Deidre, Sidney and I want you to have *this*," Catherine said, holding out a crystal ring in her small hand. "I started horseriding and Mom bought this for me at a horse show. It's too big for me right now but it will fit me when I grow older. But you have lovely delicate hands. Sidney and I want you to try it on. If it fits you, we want you to wear this ring until your ring's found."

Deidre and Harold were stunned. Deidre was the first to recover.

"Catherine, that's darling of you…but I couldn't possibly take your ring."

"Yes, you can," replied Catherine emphatically. "You are only *borrowing* it. Try it on. Please!"

Sidney stared at Deidre with his large sheepdog eyes imploring her to accept the ring.

"Catherine and Sidney can be very persistent," Lucy said with humor in her eyes. "They boss Tim and I around all the time. You must try it on."

Deidre put the ring on the third finger of her left hand.

"Oh…it looks lovely on you," Catherine said. "You *will* keep it until your ring is found," she added in a determined voice.

Deidre looked at the child and the dog. "Since you and Sidney insist, I will wear this ring with pride." She gave Catherine a hug. "Your ring will remind me of your kindness."

Tim arrived to collect the suitcases. After the luggage was packed into Harold's car, Deidre and Harold approached their hosts to thank them for their hospitality. To Sidney's annoyance, Tim kept him on a tight leash to prevent him from racing after Harold and Deidre's car in a fruitless attempt to herd them back.

When Harold approached Catherine, he knelt down on one knee as if he was paying homage to a queen. He looked up at her face.

"Catherine, thank you for lending your lovely ring to Deidre. I promise we will take good care of it. One day, when we have children of our own, I hope they will be as wonderful as you."

To the delight of everyone present, Catherine laughed with glee and gave Harold an enthusiastic hug.

CHAPTER 4

The Press Reports On The Ring's Disappearance

Later that afternoon, an anchorman turned to the camera. BREAKING NEWS appeared at the bottom of TV screens.

"Last night, a diamond engagement ring worth $50 million was stolen from the Sonoma home of Silicon Valley entrepreneur, Tim Newman. Our reporter is on the scene in Sonoma. Jennifer, what can you tell us about the latest developments in this investigation?"

A slim, attractive woman holding a TV microphone appeared on screen standing in front of the gate leading to Tim and Lucy's home.

"Gerry, the diamond ring belongs to Deidre Langton, the fiancée of famed biotech start-up entrepreneur, Harold Brewster. The police aren't giving anything away at this point in their investigation. However, we understand that this pink diamond ring is quite valuable because it was once owned by a mistress of Louis XIV."

Jennifer turned away from the camera and pointed to a large gate behind her.

"Behind me is the estate of the Sonoma home of Tim and Lucy Newman. The ring disappeared during a Crush party taking place in the wine cellar at the back of the Newman property."

"For our viewers, what's Crush, Jennifer?"

"Crush an important part of the wine making process. It takes place when wine grapes, carefully nurtured by the winemaker, finally come into the winery. Once the grapes arrive, they're immediately crushed into liquid using a large crusher machine."

"Why was Crush going on at the home of Tim Newman? Isn't he a big name in Silicon Valley tech?"

"You're correct, Gerry. Tim Newman is the CEO of the Palo Alto software company Meediya, which develops cutting-edge software for streaming entertainment data to tablets and smartphones. However, a few years back Tim Newman decided to learn firsthand about winemaking. He built a wine cellar in the back of his property and started the wine label *L'homme Nouveau*, which isn't sold commercially. The grapes are purchased from the Bartino family, a Sonoma County grower who owns a large amount of acreage in wine grapes. Once the grapes arrive, Newman and his friends crush the grapes using a large crusher machine. The ring apparently disappeared while the Newmans and their guests were busy crushing grapes."

"Any details on that?"

"We've learned that Ms. Langton took off her ring during Crush, so that it wouldn't get damaged while she was helping the other guests load grapes into the crusher. She told the police that she put the ring on a wooden ledge at the back of the wine cellar behind some wine barrels. After she'd finished loading grapes, she returned to pick up her ring only to find it missing."

"Wow, that's interesting. What do we know about the guests present at this crush?"

"Former supermodel turned vintner, Amanda Jones, was there. She's known locally for hosting rock concerts at her Sonoma Valley winery to raise money for charity. Her concerts often feature famous rock stars with whom Ms. Jones was linked socially. Her friend and international socialite, Lady Roberta Romakoff, was also present."

"I seem to have heard the name. What do we know about her?"

"According to news reports, Lady Roberta is best known for marrying well. Her title comes from her first marriage to a British Lord. She's often lambasted by the British Press for flouting social etiquette because she continues to use—or misuse—this title with her first name after remarrying twice. Her last marriage to Russian billionaire Dmitri

Romakoff ended after his "associates" tried to kidnap some British citizen in Napa Valley. According to the gossip sheets, she received a very handsome financial package from *that* divorce."

"Sounds like she's had an interesting life. Anyone else?"

"Several Silicon Valley rich and famous were also present. For example, Sand Hill Road venture capitalist Marc Todd was at Crush, along with serial entrepreneur Jason Lee and several veteran technology "grey hairs," including Tom White.

"For our viewers, please tell us what you mean by a 'technology grey hair'."

"A technology grey hair is someone with senior management experience who's brought in by the venture capitalists to advise company managers and to reassure investors when start-ups are seeking a late-stage round of venture financing, or planning to go IPO."

"Is there any word who among the guests might be prime suspects?"

"Not yet. As I said the police are keeping very quiet. However, social media is going *ballistic*."

"Tell us more."

"Users posting on Sleuths Anonymous have come up with several theories about who stole this $50 million diamond ring."

"For our viewers, what's Sleuths Anonymous?"

"Sleuths Anonymous is a social media site for amateur detectives. It encourages users to…and I quote…'get in touch with their inner Sherlock Holmes' to help solve crimes. Users who post on Sleuths Anonymous adopt tongue-in-cheek pseudonyms from famous Sherlock Holmes stories.

"Can you give us an example?"

"Gerry, let me look," replied Jennifer, staring at her handheld device. "Ah yes this is a good example: a user who's adopted the pseudonym Green Carbuncle posted on Sleuths Anonymous that Amanda Jones might profit handsomely from stealing the ring because she still moves in international high society circles and could easily sell it to one of her rich friends."

"For those viewers unfamiliar with the Sherlock Holmes mysteries, where does the pseudonym Green Carbuncle come from?"

"It's probably a reference to the Sherlock Holmes mystery *The Blue Carbuncle,* which involved the theft of a famous jewel."

"Oh, I see. Anything else?"

"Another user, Hound of Belvedere, agreed with Green Carbuncle, adding that Amanda Jones may have stolen the ring to sell it to one of the famous British rock stars who perform at the charity fundraisers held at her winery."

"Wow, I see what you mean about wild speculation. Are there other postings?"

"Nurse Watson posted that Lady Roberta Romakoff moves in similar high society circles. Therefore, *she* may have stolen the ring to sell it to one of her wealthy former husbands."

"This is beginning to sound like a TV episode from *Hollywood Wives* or *Lives of The Rich and Famous.*"

"True. However, that's not all. Other social media and several news commentators have emphasized that the hosts of the Crush party—Tim and Lucy Newman—and several Silicon Valley guests were once suspected of illegal conduct."

"Oh … that's interesting. What type of illegal conduct?"

"Unlawful insider trading."

After a long pause Jennifer continued.

"Gerry, a few years back, Tim and Lucy Newman and their guests from Silicon Valley were suspected, but not charged, with being co-conspirators in an illegal insider trading ring being run out of Mike Todd's venture capital firm on Sand Hill Road in Menlo Park. The Feds thought that these executives were providing valuable insider information about their technology companies to a group of Sonoma residents, who traded on the information and made huge profits during the Great Recession of 2008-2010. Since the tech industry was also in recession, huge profits from trading tech stocks seemed highly suspicious at the time."

"Ah … I remember this insider trading trial. Why's this relevant?"

"As I mentioned, no criminal charges were ever filed against the Silicon Valley executives. However, amateur sleuths on Sleuths Anonymous are now digging up all the dirt they can find about this insider trading case and trying to connect it to this missing diamond ring."

"Can you give us an example?"

The female reporter quickly checked her device and looked back at the camera.

"Dancing Man posted that four Sonoma residents previously charged with illegal insider trading were *also* present when this valuable pink diamond ring disappeared.

"Oh, I see. For our viewers who may not be familiar with this previous trial, who were these four Sonoma residents?"

"Bob Goodwin, a well-known caterer, Peter Smith, a tasting room employee, Samantha Pond, a local Realtor, and Charlie Bartino, a member of the renowned Sonoma County grape growing family."

"What were these four individuals doing at the Crush party?"

"Samantha Pond was a guest. Bob Goodman catered the event. Peter Smith poured wine, and Charlie Bartino delivered the grapes. Dancing Man theorized that he sees a common pattern of criminal behavior because, in his words, 'illegal insider trading and stealing diamond rings are crimes motivated by *greed*.'"

"Hmmm, maybe, but I don't see the connection between someone who might have engaged in illegal insider trading and someone who steals a valuable diamond ring. Seems to me those crimes involve very different skills and contacts. Anything else?"

"Twisted Lip posted a reply to Dancing Man that Charlie Bartino and Tom White are well known collectors of expensive military hardware from World War II and Korea. Twisted Lip suggested that these collectors may also collect famous jewels sold on the black market or the Dark Web."

"These postings all sounds crazy to me. Do the police have any leads to suspects who might have stolen this diamond?"

"As I mentioned earlier, the police are keeping very quiet about their investigation. However, we understand the authorities have not ruled out anyone as a suspect. The entire list of guests and people present on the scene of the crime are under investigation."

"Ok Jennifer, we'll get back to you later."

The screen returned to the anchorman.

"We now go to one of our experts, a former federal prosecutor William Reed to give us some insight about how a criminal investigation of this nature might develop. Bill Reed, can you tell our viewers how this type of case normally proceeds?"

A handsome, stern-faced lawyer replaced the anchorman onscreen.

"Gerry, in my experience, several local, state, and national agencies are already involved in this investigation. Bank accounts will be carefully monitored. Agents will be shadowing the diamond market to see if anything suspicious shows up."

"Given the celebrity guest list and this particular diamond's value, would you expect any *international* agencies to be involved?"

"Sure. By now, our US authorities, including the CIA and Interpol will have notified the international diamond market about this disappearance. This famous diamond was recently sold at auction in London. The diamond markets in London and elsewhere have to be on the lookout for this ring."

"If that's the case, how is it possible for anyone to sell it?"

"Unfortunately, a deep black market exists in trading valuable antiques and gemstones. A wealthy private collector might buy this diamond from the thief and keep it hidden for decades. The diamond may end up in a country or jurisdiction which refuses to cooperate with US authorities in tracking down international villains. Anything's possible."

"So, in fact there *is* a black market for such a valuable diamond as suggested on social media?"

"Yes, indeed," replied the lawyer.

CHAPTER 5

Sidney Begins His Investigation

A few days later, Lucy Newman sat with attorney Ann Schiller in the Newman's Sonoma sitting room. Sidney lay nearby looking adoringly at both beautiful blonde women.

"Lucy, I'm so sorry this happened," Ann said, looking with horror and sympathy at her hostess. "I'd hoped to be useful by contacting my former colleagues at Justice for some inside scoop on the investigation. I've also tried to contact the Sonoma County Sherriff's Department. So far, no one's returned my calls. How is everything with you and Tim? I saw the press hanging around outside your gate when I drove in."

Lucy shook her head in dismay. "Ann...it's been a *nightmare*. When we're in Sonoma, the press camps outside our home here. When we're in Palo Alto, the press camps outside our home there. They're also camping outside Tim's workplace, as if that will solve anything. I've had to stop going to the gym because the press follows me and interviews other gym members while I'm working out."

"People caught up in a criminal investigation always have a difficult time. Any idea as to what may have happened?"

"Ever since the ring's disappearance, I've been trying to figure out *who* would have taken it. Tim and I know it wasn't us. But it's horrible suspecting our closest friends. *They* probably suspect *us*."

"Some of your friends are higher up on the list of suspects than others," Ann replied. "People are posting a ton of garbage about my aunt Amanda and her friend Lady Roberta on Sleuths Anonymous. The TV channels and newspapers are gleefully digging up decades-old stories about my aunt's former life as a supermodel, including her celebrity rock star boyfriends. Lady Roberta's wealthy ex-husbands have all been profiled in the news. It's pretty disgusting."

Sidney stood up suddenly. A rare note of emotion had crept into Ann's otherwise cool calm voice. He went over to sit by her feet and put a large paw on her lap.

Ann began stroking Sidney behind his ears. "It's OK big guy. You don't have to protect me. I'm not the one in trouble."

"Sidney's very sensitive," Lucy said, watching her sheepdog lovingly. "He knows when we're upset."

Ann nodded. "Talking of being upset, everyone who attended your crush event is lawyering up. Harold Brewster's a corporate client of our firm. My colleague Phil Taylor introduced Harold to Tracy Sanchez, a former federal prosecutor who works in our Palo Alto office. Tracy represented Harold during the recent police interviews. My aunt Amanda's asked her longtime friend, George De Rosa, to represent her after the police came knocking at her door. With social media throwing around outlandish theories, no one's taking any chances."

"Tim and I hired our lawyer, Lillian Johnson, to represent us in the recent police and FBI grillings," Lucy replied.

"Oh, I remember Lillian," Ann replied. "She represented you guys when you were subpoenaed to testify in the insider trading trial a few years back. Does Lillian know I'm here? If not, I need to check that she's OK with this."

"Don't worry, Ann," Lucy smiled. "I've already told Lillian that you'd be coming by. She trusts you and agrees that we don't want to be completely shut away from everyone. It's lonely enough as it is. However, she did ask me to find out if you'd managed to learn anything about the investigation from your old pals in the Justice Department."

Ann laughed. "That sounds like Lillian. George also suggested that I contact my former colleagues. Unfortunately, as I mentioned earlier the crowd at Justice is keeping its mouth shut. They're no doubt aware that

Harold's represented by my firm and my aunt's a possible suspect."

"Ann, if you were still a federal prosecutor at the US Attorney's office, what would you suspect had happened to this diamond ring?" Lucy asked anxiously.

"Good question! I didn't handle high-profile theft cases when I worked at Justice in San Francisco. However, Tracy Sanchez handled several cases involving stolen fine art and jewelry when she worked for Justice in Miami. Unfortunately, Tracy thinks is that this valuable pink diamond has probably been sold to a wealthy collector, which supports those nasty theories about my aunt and Lady Roberta being posted on Sleuths Anonymous. Another possibility is it's been chopped up and sold on the black market."

"Oh no! That would be a tragedy. It's such a lovely ring. The diamond is so beautiful … and the setting is gorgeous."

Listening to the conversation, Sidney began to worry. *"Sounds like the trail's gone cold. With Ann's help, I must persuade Mom to let me into the wine cellar."*

Sidney went over and stared at Lucy. He swiftly ran to the French windows. He returned again and stared at Lucy.

"What going on, big guy?" Ann asked.

"He probably wants to go outside," Lucy said turning her attention to the large sheepdog who looked at her imploringly. "In fact, while you're here, would you like to see the scene of the crime?"

"Sure, if you don't mind."

"Oh good. Mum's taking Ann to see the cellar. She'll finally let me in!"

Lucy opened the French windows. Sidney rushed outside to the huge barn doors of the wine cellar. He stood staring at the doors, whimpering that he wanted to go inside.

Lucy laughed and shook her head. "Sidney's been bugging me to let him into the wine cellar ever since the night of the Crush party. Now that the police have finished their search for clues and the wine making tools have been stored away, I can safely let him in."

Lucy opened the huge barn doors and the sheepdog rushed in. He carefully sniffed around the walls of the barn. He began exploring the area where the grapes were crushed.

"*Darn…everything smells too clean. Wait a minute. I think I detect Deidre's scent,*" Sidney thought to himself. "*I'll see if I can follow it.*"

"Look, Ann," Lucy said excitedly. "Sidney's sniffing the ground in the area where we loaded grapes into the crusher. What a clever dog," she said admiringly.

Ann and Lucy followed Sidney, who was sniffing the floor carefully. "Wow…he's slowly sniffing his way to the back of the cellar," Lucy said excitedly. "That's where the ring disappeared."

The sheepdog stopped walking and looked up at several wooden barrels stacked against the back wall. He squeezed his large body in between the barrels to sniff a wooden ledge attached to the back wall.

"Goodness! Sidney is sniffing the exact spot where Deidre told us she'd hidden her ring." Lucy stopped smiling. "Deidre thought her ring would be safely out of the way on a ledge behind one of these barrels. I still can't believe the ring just vanished. It was so far away from the area where we were all crushing the grapes."

Ann put a consoling hand on Lucy's shoulder.

"Lucy, while you were crushing the grapes, could someone walk back to this area without being seen?"

"Sure! This area is very dark at night. Deidre thought her ring would be out of harm's way because none of Crush was going on back here. We were all busy taking turns throwing grapes into the crusher. Deidre never thought someone would steal her ring. She's a very trusting person."

After Ann peered at the ledge and wooden barrels, she moved away.

"Lucy, would anyone have noticed if someone took a short break and walked back here?"

"No," Lucy replied after a brief hesitation. "I have to be honest about that. We all took turns throwing grapes into the crusher. However, we couldn't all throw the grapes into the crusher at the same time. Most of the time, we stood around waiting our turn. We were all very focused on getting Crush over as quickly as possible. None of us would've noticed if someone took a short break and walked to the back of the cellar."

Lucy sighed deeply. "Ann … there's something else I haven't told anyone. After the police arrived and we returned to the house, Harold got into an argument with Deidre. He said she'd been stupid and accused everyone else of stealing the ring. Deidre naturally got upset and ran to one of our bathrooms for a tissue. After I followed her, she confided to me that she was so shaken and upset that she couldn't be 100% sure where she put her ring. I haven't mentioned this to anyone because I don't want to create problems for Deidre if she has to testify in court. I learned firsthand during that horrible insider trading trial how ordinary people get nervous as hell when they get caught up in a criminal trial. At one point, while I was waiting outside the courtroom before being called to testify, I became so scared that I thought I'd forget my own name."

Ann smiled sympathetically at Lucy. "I understand." However, Ann secretly began to question Deidre's veracity. *"How the heck could anyone forget where she put a $50 million diamond ring?"* Ann thought to herself.

Sidney continued to sniff around the floor and walls where the barrels were stored. He stopped and put his nose in the air.

"Deidre definitely walked over here…but so have several other humans." An Aussie pout appeared on his face. *"Since I wasn't allowed into the wine cellar until now, it's difficult to distinguish the individual scent of the thief at this late stage. Ah … wait a minute. I smell bay leaf. Maybe it's the scent of a toilet product used by the thief."*

Sidney continued pacing around the barrels.

"I also smell another scent. It's too strong to be human but it isn't as strong as the scent of my wildlife pals who sleep rough, like the squirrels."

After Sidney finished sniffing around the back wall, he looked up at the cellar ceiling and sighed.

"I must find this animal or bird. It may have seen what happened to Deidre's ring the night it disappeared."

CHAPTER 6

More Social Media Theories

An anchorman turned to the camera. BREAKING NEWS appeared at the bottom of TV screens.

"As we previously reported, a diamond ring worth $50 million was stolen from the Sonoma home of Silicon Valley CEO Tim Newman. The valuable ring went missing during a Crush party that took place in a wine cellar located at the back of the Newman property. Our reporter is on the scene in Sonoma. Jennifer, what can you tell us about the latest developments in this investigation?"

A female reporter appeared onscreen. "Gerry, I'm standing in front of the local police station of the Sonoma County Sherriff's Department in the City of Sonoma. The police have been silent on the matter so far. However, we've learned that the insurance company that insured this valuable diamond ring hasn't paid the insurance claim filed by Harold Brewster, who purchased the ring for fianceé Deidre Langton...yet."

"Any reason given for the delay?"

"We understand from the spokesperson for the insurance company that any delay in paying this claim is due to the high value of the diamond ring and the fact that the police haven't completed their investigation into its disappearance."

"Any word from the police regarding who's still on their list of suspects or persons of interest?"

"No word yet but we understand that no one who attended the Crush party has been *removed* as a suspect."

"Anything else?"

"The spokesperson for the insurance company also informed us that they've started their own independent investigation, which she assured us is standard procedure for this type of claim. Off the record, we have learned that the insurance company will *not* pay this claim until *both* the police investigation *and* the insurance company's own independent investigation are complete."

"Do we know anything else about this diamond's disappearance? What's the latest buzz in social media on this?"

"Gerry, postings on Sleuths Anonymous are weighing in on these developments, as you would expect. The posts have commented at length that the police don't seem to be getting anywhere. All sorts of conspiracy theories are being thrashed out."

"Tell us more."

"Several posts on Sleuths Anonymous speculate that one or more of the executives from Silicon Valley may have stolen the ring because they are about to lose their jobs."

"Wait a minute. That sounds crazy to me. Why would anyone from Silicon Valley be laid off? Isn't the area booming right now?"

Jennifer reviewed her device.

"Mr. Hudson posted that some tech sectors, such as The Internet of Things, aren't generating the revenues and growth expected by their investors. Private investment money may be drying up.

"Another poster, Techie Thumb agreed with Mr. Hudson, adding that it's impossible to know what's really going on inside most start-ups because many delay going IPO, which would require public financials. Techie Thumb also posted that the gossip around Silicon Valley is that many start-ups aren't generating enough revenue to be self-sufficient without serious cash infusions. Therefore, if private investment dries up in these sectors, start-ups and their investors could be hit hard."

"If this gossip is true, do any of the Silicon Valley guys who attended the Crush party work at any of these potentially vulnerable start-ups?"

Jennifer again checked her handheld.

"One of the Silicon Valley guests, Tom White is currently working for a start-up in the Internet of Things sector. He was recruited to work there by another guest at Crush, venture capitalist Marc Todd, whose firm is heavily invested in this start-up. Apparently, this company is trying to secure a critical round of financing. Techie Thumb posted that Tom White might be out of a job if this new round of financing doesn't happen."

"Wow, that's interesting."

"Serial entrepreneur Jason Lee is also working for a new start-up. He might be vulnerable if there's a sudden tech downturn."

"But Jennifer, we understand that these guys are reportedly very affluent. Sounds like they can afford to be out of work for a bit."

"True. However other Sleuths Anonymous posts also claim that these Silicon Valley guys maintain a very high standard of living, including ownership of expensive homes in Silicon Valley *and* wine country. They're all early stage investors, so they might be financially vulnerable in a serious downturn."

"Hmm, I'm skeptical that any of the Silicon Valley guests stole the ring. Even if they're early stage investors, they must have made a killing during the recent tech boom. They probably can sit out a few early stage investments going sour. What about our high-profile female guests?"

"Some posts continue to focus on the international socialites—Lady Roberta Romakoff and Amanda Jones—who were there."

"Tell us more."

"Nurse Watson wondered whether Lady Roberta Romakoff's divorce proceedings were properly finalized before she remarried. This post suggested that Lady Roberta may have stolen the ring because she's being blackmailed for being a bigamist."

"That sounds *very* far-fetched to me. What's social media now saying about Amanda Jones?"

"Gerry, as you may recall, Amanda Jones is a former British supermodel turned Sonoma vintner. Hound of Belvedere continues to focus on her as the main suspect because this amateur sleuth thinks that many Brits have 'sticky fingers' ... meaning other people's belongings stick to their fingers.

"Green Carbuncle posted that the gossip around Sonoma is that Amanda Jones and Lady Roberta showed an inordinate amount of interest in this valuable ring at the Crush party. Another post by Orange Pips demanded that Amanda Jones be immediately locked up because she might head back to Britain."

"These theories sound highly speculative, especially the suggestion that Amanda Jones is a flight risk. She's got a lot of money tied up here. Jennifer, thanks for your report."

The anchorman turned to face the TV screen.

"If you've just tuned in to this program, we are reporting on the disappearance of a famous diamond ring worth $50 million from the Sonoma home of Silicon Valley CEO Tim Newman during a Crush party.

"The police have not revealed anything except that everyone who attended the event is a suspect. We've also reported that the insurance company that insured this expensive diamond ring has not—and I repeat *not*—paid anything out on this claim.

"Several amateur detectives on the social media platform Sleuths Anonymous have come up with wild and outlandish theories as to why certain guests at the Crush party might have a motive to steal this valuable ring. To keep you informed, we've added their posts to our social media platforms on Facebook and twitter.

"The police investigation into the disappearance of this diamond is ongoing. We promise to keep you up-to-date on the latest developments. Please follow us on Facebook and twitter so we can continue to bring you the latest news on the mysterious disappearance of this diamond ring in Sonoma, California."

CHAPTER 7

Sidney Appears Before The Sonoma Wildlife Council

Sidney waited patiently for the Sonoma Wildlife Council to convene. A large mountain lion stealthily arrived to preside over the group. After noting Sidney's presence, the mountain lion shook his enormous head with exasperation.

"Sidney Newman, kindly step forward to address our council. However, I must warn you that we will not look kindly on any request to grant you permission to enter our protected wildlife habitat. On one occasion we granted you access to one of our trails and you were the cause of an ugly, loud helicopter's arrival that nearly frightened us to death."

"G'day, Mr. President and all the members of the Wildlife Council of the great City of Sonoma," said Sidney proudly. *"I'm not seeking permission to enter any wildlife trails. Instead, I need your help to find a wild animal or bird that recently visited my human Dad's wine cellar. I think this wild creature may have been in the wine cellar on the night a valuable $50 million diamond engagement ring was stolen."*

The mountain lion looked skeptical. "Sidney, as a pampered domestic animal, you must understand that members of the Sonoma Wildlife Council and our constituents have to fight every day for our very survival. You want us to be concerned about the loss of a $50 million engagement ring?"

"Mr. President, I know this missing ring must seem trivial to any member of this council. But humans are different from us. They place value on things that we know are unimportant, like this ring. They can't help themselves; they're only human.

"The big problem is that my humans Lucy and Tim and all their guests

and catering staff are suspected of stealing this jewel. If my humans are wrongly convicted of this crime and sent to jail, I will lose my home and family. I may be thrown out on the streets without any of the survival skills that you brilliant wildlife council members learn from birth."

"Hmmm. OK, Sidney. Flattery will get you nowhere, but we now understand why you may need our help. But first, why do you think that a member of our wildlife community visited your human's wine cellar?" The mountain lion asked judicially.

"Using my sheepdog nose, I detected the scent of a wild animal or bird in the area of the cellar where the jewel was last seen. I need to find out if this creature was in the cellar when the theft occurred and whether it can provide any information that might lead me to identify the thief."

"We acknowledge that you sheepdogs have an excellent sense of smell," noted the mountain lion. "However, I don't see why our council has to get involved in this human problem. Does any other representative present have an opinion on this matter?"

A tiny California towhee spoke up.

"Mr. President, Sidney's humans are very kind to us birds. Their daughter Catherine puts out food and water in our bird feeders all year 'round. During the winter months, she saves many of us from starvation. I'd like this council to help Sidney if we can."

"I second that," said the California scrub jay representative, who was busy removing ticks and other annoying parasites from the back of the deer representative.

The deer representative raised her head and looked at the group with her lovely brown eyes. "Jays help us deer remove pesky ticks off our backs that we can't reach. If our jay representative says we should support Sidney – then I agree."

"Well I can't see how we can help," the mountain lion sighed. "They'll kill me if I go anywhere near a human neighborhood. Sidney, what exactly are you suggesting?"

"Mr. President, I would never request that you personally appear below your habitat. But could you and the other council members notify the Sonoma wildlife community that I'm trying to find an animal or bird that recently visited my human Dad's wine cellar? It's possible that this creature lives in my neighborhood."

"Could this creature be a cat?" asked the deer representative. "I often see cats chasing rats and mice on your neighborhood."

Sidney tilted his head to one side as he tried to remember the scent in the cellar. "This creature's scent was not the scent of a cat," he replied. "It wasn't strong, like the scent of a raccoon or a skunk. I seem to recall the scent of bay leaves, but this could have been from human soap or another toiletry item."

While the animals and birds listened to Sidney, a large red-shouldered hawk flew by and came to rest on a tall tree. The mountain lion roared to interrupt the discussion.

"Members of the Sonoma Wildlife Council, we are privileged to have a member of the Avian Highway Patrol join us today. Officer Hawk has graciously offered give us advice on how we wildlife can avoid becoming road kill."

The mountain lion turned to the hawk.

"Officer Hawk, we know your time is precious but this domestic sheepdog, Sidney Newman, has requested our help in tracing a wild animal or bird that may have witnessed the disappearance of a shiny bauble highly valued by the humans. Do you have any words of wisdom for us regarding this matter?"

From a nearby tall tree, the Avian Highway Patrol officer looked down on the group below with a fierce expression. "Before I can offer any advice, I must first learn the circumstances surrounding this trinket's disappearance."

Sidney became excited. "Officer Hawk, the theft occurred in a cellar at my home about a week ago. The human police suspect that someone present at a Crush party stole a valuable pink diamond ring worth $50 million. I can give you a description of the ring and all the humans who were present when the ring disappeared."

"I'll fly by your home to get a full description of this ring and those present during its disappearance. And I'll notify the members of my Avian Highway

Patrol to watch out for these humans and any baubles fitting the description of this ring."

The mountain lion decided to take charge of the meeting. *'Thank you, Officer Hawk."* He turned to Sidney. *"OK, Sidney, our Sonoma Wildlife Council will ask their constituents to contact Officer Hawk if they've observed any wild creature entering or leaving your human Dad's wine cellar. However, we must move on. We have a long agenda before us."*

Officer Hawk began his speech. *"Members of the Sonoma Wildlife Council, you must warn your constituents that humans are too wrapped up in their own affairs to pay much attention to us wildlife. They're always in a hurry. They drive at high speeds on our county roads, as if they're on the Sears Point racetrack. Our Avian Highway Patrol frequently observe humans talking on their cell phones while driving fast. Sometimes we see humans staring at their phones ... not at the road ahead. Since they're not watching out for us, we end up as road kill."*

Sidney knew he was dismissed from the Sonoma Wildlife Council.

CHAPTER 8

Social Media Suspects The Victims

An anchorman turned to the camera. BREAKING NEWS again appeared at the bottom of TV screens.

"As we previously reported, a diamond ring worth $50 million was stolen from the Sonoma home of famed Silicon Valley entrepreneur, Tim Newman. Our reporter is on the scene in Sonoma. Jennifer, what can you tell us about the latest developments in this investigation?"

A female reporter appeared onscreen. "Gerry, I don't have anything new to report from the police. I'm standing in front of the residence of Harold Brewster in Palo Alto. New postings on Sleuths Anonymous now speculate that the *victims* of the theft, Harold Brewster and his fiancée Deidre Langton, might have stolen the ring themselves."

"Why should anyone think that the victims stole their own ring?"

"Gerry, it's important to emphasize to our viewers that this is all social media speculation at this point. However, Purple-Headed League posted that Harold Brewster may have planned to collect the insurance money *and* keep the ring … or sell it to one of his wealthy Silicon Valley associates.

"Wow, that's quite damning. Any evidence to support this accusation?"

"Bohemian Dude posted a reply that Harold Brewster's fiancée, Ms. Langton, acted very suspiciously when she left this valuable ring on a ledge at the back of the cellar during Crush."

"I'm sure Ms. Langton now regrets that she didn't put the ring in a safer place. However, I'm not convinced that this is evidence that she or her fiancée committed the theft. Anything else?"

"Not at this time … but we'll be constantly checking social media to see what else is posted."

"Hey Dude, you should read what they're saying on Sleuths Anonymous about Harold Brewster," said the young man staring at his screen. He turned to face his boss. "Wasn't he your boss at one time? Didn't you work for his start-up before it was acquired?"

"Yeah, I worked for Harold Brewster," replied the second man, leaving his computer to peer over the young man's shoulder. "Damn glad I don't work for him anymore."

"Did you make a killing on your stock options?"

The older man winced. "I got out before my options vested."

"Too bad. Still it's interesting what's being said about this guy and his fiancée."

"No kidding," the older man replied. He returned to his computer and searched for Sleuths Anonymous. He smiled when he read the postings on the disappearance of the diamond ring. "Hey gang, I really like this platform. It's a great way to get the word out about scumbags like Harold Brewster. I think we should all sign up, so we get notified whenever someone posts new info about this missing ring. After work, I'll share what I know about Brewster that will make us all LOL."

"Can't wait," the younger man yelled. Most of the older man's software team nodded their heads in agreement.

A woman working nearby didn't join in the frivolity. "I expect my boss will start bullying this guy Brewster—like he bullies me," she thought to herself.

Later that evening, a poster using the pseudonym Swamp Adder appeared on Sleuths Anonymous. The follow morning an anchorman turned to the camera.

"Our reporter now brings us the latest about the $50 million diamond ring stolen in Sonoma. Jennifer, tell us about these latest developments."

"Gerry, I'm again standing in front of the residence of Harold Brewster in Palo Alto. As we reported yesterday, postings on Sleuths Anonymous by Purple-Headed League and Bohemian Dude speculated that the *victims* of the theft, Harold Brewster and his fiancée Deidre Langton, might have stolen the ring themselves. Last night, a new amateur sleuth using the pseudonym Swamp Adder agreed with Purple-Headed League and Bohemian Dude that Harold Brewster had the most to gain by stealing the ring. However, Swamp Adder posted a very different theory about the theft.

"Tell us more."

"Swamp Adder wrote that he has…and I quote…'personal knowledge that Harold Brewster is dishonest and has a secret lover.' "

"Interesting! Do you have further details, Jennifer?"

The female reporter turned to her handheld.

"Swamp Adder's post reads as follows: 'I'm personally familiar with the career of this dishonest, narcissistic entrepreneur. I and many others in Silicon Valley suspect that Harold Brewster faked the initial lab work and animal testing needed to obtain Fast Track FDA approval for his UTI vaccine.' "

"Hold on a moment…what's this UTI vaccine?"

"It's the vaccine that Harold Brewster developed to combat urinary tract infections in seniors. The discovery of this vaccine made Mr. Brewster famous because UTI in seniors can cause serious problems, such as sudden loss of mobility or dementia.' "

"I see. Does the post say anything else?"

"Yes, it goes on to state 'I and many others in Silicon Valley also suspect that Brewster faked his company's financials during the acquisition of his lucrative start-up by big pharma. Faking lab tests and company financials is typical Brewster behavior.'"

"Wow, those are wild accusations. Does the post say anything else about the secret lover?"

"Yes, Swamp Adder's post goes on to say 'Before the diamond disappeared, I personally observed Harold Brewster having lunch in Woodside with a very attractive woman, who is *not* his fiancée. This woman was dressed in a tight skirt and high heels and leaned over Brewster with written materials, as if they were conspiring about something. Maybe Harold stole the ring to give it to his new girlfriend? If so, this would explain why his fiancée didn't sell her San Carlos condo after she moved in with Brewster.' Gerry, that's the post by Swamp Adder."

"This beats the soaps, Jennifer. And we should remind our viewers that the content of these posts from social media are wholly unverifiable. For those viewers who are unfamiliar with the Sherlock Holmes mysteries, where does the pseudonym Swamp Adder come from?"

"I think it's a reference to the Sherlock Holmes mystery, The Speckled Band. In that mystery, a deadly adder was trained to slither down a bell rope and fatally bite two young women while they were in bed asleep."

"Charming story!" the anchorman exclaimed.

Turning to face the camera, the anchor added, "Well that's all we have for you tonight. Please continue to follow us on Facebook and twitter as we bring you the latest news and social media theories on the mysterious disappearance of this $50 million diamond ring."

CHAPTER 9

Harold Brewster Visits His Lawyers

Harold Brewster was furious with the criminal accusations on social media about him and Deidre. After arriving via Uber, he sat fuming in the waiting room of the Palo Alto office of Horace & Fitzgerald, a prominent international law firm.

"Hey, man! Good to see you," Phil Taylor, a tall, dark-haired corporate lawyer greeted Harold. "Come into this conference room. I'll introduce you to our Libel Law specialist, Bertrand Wainwright, from our San Francisco office.

"Harold, pleased to meet you," said the grey-haired lawyer wearing a tweed sports jacket and bow tie who entered the conference room seconds later. After everyone was seated with coffee or sparkling water, Wainwright asked, "How can we help?"

Harold glared at both lawyers. "I don't know if you've been following the news recently, but some jerks on Sleuths Anonymous are accusing me and my fiancée Deidre of stealing her diamond engagement ring, which is preposterous."

Bertrand Wainwright raised one eyebrow. "I'm unfamiliar with the platform, Sleuths Anonymous. Tell me more."

"Wait, I've got the posts here," Harold said as he reached into his rucksack and pulled out his laptop. "If you give me your Wi-Fi info, I'll send them to you."

Phil gave Harold the firm's guest Wi-Fi and the lawyers left to retrieve their laptops.

"OK, the posts are on their way," Harold told the lawyers as they returned to the table.

"While we're booting up our laptops, clue me in on Sleuths Anonymous," Bertrand requested.

Harold stroked his long brown rectangular beard. "Sleuths Anonymous is used by amateur, wannabe sleuths to post theories about who committed high-profile crimes using silly pseudonyms from Sherlock Holmes stories. After Deidre's ring disappeared, a bunch of dumb idiots with too much time on their hands used this platform to share their theories about the thief's identity. At first, these posts nailed some of the other guests at the Crush party. However, a recent post by Purple-Headed League suggested that I stole the ring as part of a plot to collect the insurance money and keep the ring or sell it to one of my wealthy Silicon Valley buddies."

"Hmmm, that's interesting," Bertrand replied. "Any facts cited to back up that accusation?"

"Nope," replied Harold. "Take a look. It's the first attachment I sent you."

"Ah…I just received your email," Phil said. "Wow this is really something," he added after opening the attachments to read.

"As you will see, another f---r using the pseudonym Bohemian Dude posted that Deidre's behavior at the Crush party was 'very suspicious.'"

The lawyers quietly reviewed the posts while Harold continued to vent.

"Another bastard using the pseudonym Swamp Adder claimed to have personal knowledge that I'm dishonest, have a secret lover on the side, and everyone in Silicon Valley suspects me of faking my startup's financials and FDA submissions. Phil…you and the other lawyers in this office know damn well *that's not true.*"

"That's correct," replied Phil looking up from his laptop. "Guys, it seems to me that the outrageous accusations by the third poster, Swamp Adder, are easily refutable," Phil said calmly. He turned to face Bertrand.

"Harold's one of our most successful start-up clients. From the very beginning, we figured out that his start-up's UTI vaccine was marketable worldwide. We've worked closely with his company from its initial financing to its lucrative sale. We may be able to quickly come up with expert auditors who will verify that these claims are complete garbage."

"Let me carefully reread this Swamp Adder posting," Bertrand said in a cautious tone of voice. "It's much longer than the others."

Harold stood up and stared out the window. He turned around to face the lawyers.

"I don't know where these shitheads get their crazy ideas. I didn't steal the ring and I don't have any love interest apart from Deidre."

Bertrand looked up from reading the email. "Harold, we believe you…trust me," he replied trying to calm Harold down.

"Yeah man, it's the pits," Phil shook his head in disgust.

"What really ticks me off is that these posts weren't noticed by anyone until a couple of TV and radio stations started fraud-casting this crap to their viewers and listeners."

"Ah, that's actually pretty typical," Bertrand nodded his head.

"Several newspapers started piling on by adding these posts to their news reports about Deidre's missing ring. Obviously, they're using these vicious posts to improve ratings and circulation—at the expense of me and Deidre."

"Very likely," Bertrand said. "I'll have my paralegal retrieve all the press reports about these posts. How's your fiancée taking all this?"

"Fortunately, Deidre believed me when I assured her that I'm not dating another woman on the side. But the look in her eyes when she reads this crap makes me want to kill someone."

Harold returned to the table and slumped down in his chair. After a long pause, during which Harold gulped down his glass of water, he looked up at the lawyers.

"I'm going to sue all these bastards for slandering us in this hateful way. I'm going to sue Sleuths Anonymous for providing these lying bastards a platform to spread lies about us. I want you lawyers to investigate and find out who the f---s are who spread these malicious lies. Once I find out who they are, I'll sue the bastards and ruin them. I'll also sue the press to teach them not to fraud-cast this crap."

Bertrand looked sympathetically at Harold. "Unfortunately, Harold, you are not alone in being badmouthed online. I've heard numerous similar stories from other clients. I'm happy to review the most recent case law pertaining to these posts and the role played by the mainstream press in republishing these falsehoods. However, I must advise you from the outset that US libel cases are notoriously difficult to win."

Harold slunk even deeper in his chair with a long sigh. The lawyer continued.

"Our legal right to sue someone who libels or slanders us frequently collides with our legal right to free speech under the First Amendment. In recent years, the Internet triggered new law that makes libel lawsuits very challenging for plaintiffs.

As Harold murmured, "Oh, Christ" under his breath the lawyer continued.

"For example, Section 230 (c)(1) of the Federal Communications Decency Act provides a social media platform like Sleuths Anonymous complete immunity from liability for libelous statements posted by its users *if the platform was the information content provider* and others provided the content. This Section could enable Sleuths Anonymous to kick a libel lawsuit out of court if the court finds that Sleuths Anonymous was an information content provider at the time the statements were posted and the libelous statements were solely provided by the users of Sleuths Anonymous, and not Sleuths Anonymous."

"That's ridiculous!" Harold exploded. "Does that mean I can't sue *anyone* for posting this crap?"

"No, this Act only protects the *platforms*, not the users who post material on the platforms. Some want this Section reformed to make the platforms more accountable for what's being posted on them. However, the way Congress works, we shouldn't hold our breath that this will occur anytime soon," Bertrand added with a grim expression.

"I also understand your desire to sue the anonymous users who posted these outrageous allegations against you and your fiancée. But before they're added to any libel lawsuit, we need to discover their *true* identities."

"I thought you guys knew how to do all that," Harold said, shocked.

"Obviously, we're quite adept at subpoenaing platforms like Sleuths Anonymous for any and all information about their users," Bertrand replied. "However, it's quite common for these platforms to oppose our subpoenas. They almost always want to protect the anonymous identity of their users. If Sleuths Anonymous opposes our subpoena, the court will protect the anonymous posters' identities from disclosure unless we can show that the postings were *clearly* libelous."

"Oh, for god's sake. Of course they were libelous," Harold shouted at the lawyer.

"Perhaps," replied Bertrand kindly. "However, the California Court of Appeal has issued several rulings that wild and crazy posts on the Internet may *not* be libelous if the reasonable reader wouldn't take these posts seriously. As I said earlier, I need to carefully analyze these posts to see whether they're protected speech pursuant to these rulings." Before Harold could explode again, Bertrand continued.

"Even if we force Sleuths Anonymous to cooperate with our subpoena, we may still face problems suing individuals who have libeled you."

"Why?" Harold demanded belligerently.

"Yes, Bertrand, I'm also puzzled," Phil added. "Once Sleuths Anonymous hands over its information about these users, why would you have a problem adding them to the lawsuit?" Bertrand paused for several seconds before replying.

"As I'm sure you're both aware, there is a certain type of anonymous user online who takes great pleasure in posting outrageous statements about prominent people, like Harold."

"That's probably true," Harold reluctantly acknowledged. "There are a lot of jerks out there who like to throw shit at anyone who's successful."

"Exactly! Here's the problem with information obtained from a platform like Sleuths Anonymous. Many social media users go to great lengths to conceal their identity. The type of individual who, in your words, Harold, 'likes to throw shit at anyone who's successful' is just the type of individual who will lie outright about their true identity to a platform like Sleuths."

"Oh, I see." Phil slowly nodded his head as Harold groaned.

"This means that we can fight like hell to get Sleuths Anonymous to give up information about these users only to discover the information about the user's identity is as bogus as the user's posts." Bertrand paused to let the bad news sink in before he continued.

"I also sympathize with Harold's desire to sue broadcasters and newspapers that republished the posts. However, in the early 1990s, California passed the first Anti-SLAPP Act designed to protect freedom of speech in the age of the Internet. This statute requires all plaintiffs suing for libel to provide early proof that the lawsuit is *likely to prevail*. Otherwise, the court will dismiss the libel lawsuit and order the plaintiff to pay defense legal fees and costs."

The room went silent as Harold and Phil pondered the lawyer's advice. Bertrand spoke first.

"Harold, it's entirely your decision whether you proceed to court, but bringing a libel suit is complicated. Many of our most successful, prominent clients get hammered unfairly in social media. We don't always recommend that clients sue for libel." Bertrand closed his computer. "Before you make a final decision, I want you to read a law review article written by my department. It provides an overview of current US libel law as it impacts social media. I'll also send you a piece that offers alternatives for combatting social media falsehoods *other than* filing a libel lawsuit."

"I also want to sue my insurance company," Harold said, ignoring Bertrand's words of caution. "That damned company is also damaging our reputations by not immediately paying our insurance claim."

Phil raised his hand, signaling Bertrand to speak. "Harold, unfortunately, we may not be able to help you there. Our firm represents several excess insurance carriers, so we may have a conflict. However, we can refer you to a couple of top notch law firms handling that type of lawsuit."

"Everyone keeps telling me that I face an uphill battle suing these bastards... *even you guys*," Harold said as he snapped his screen closed. "But the important people in the Silicon Valley know that I *never* run away from a fight."

"I've told Deidre that it's not right for these bastards to smear our names and drag us through the mud without any comeuppance or consequence," he added as he sat, arms crossed and glaring at the lawyers. "Phil's mentioned the worldwide impact of the UTI vaccine that my start-up discovered and monetized. However, what Phil *doesn't* know is that I started the quest to discover this vaccine because I saw my grandfather *humiliated* in his final years by an undetected urinary tract infection. That UTI caused an otherwise healthy and active man to immediately lose the use of his legs and suffer the onset of dementia. His idiot doctors all claimed—and treated him for—a stroke he never had. Only much later did they get it right. By then it was too late to reverse the evil impact of this UTI."

"Wow, that's terrible," Phil leaned forward.

"Watching my grandfather, a brilliant scientist, suffer the loss of his mental faculties during his final years made me work damned hard to discover a UTI vaccine so other seniors wouldn't suffer the same humiliation." Harold uncrossed his arms and ran his fingers through his hair in exasperation.

"OK…people can sneer all they want about how my vaccine made me rich. However, that's *not* why I worked so hard to develop it. After coming up with a solution to a very nasty problem that can impact any of us in our final years, I'll be damned if I sit back and let those shitheads humiliate me and Deidre with their lies.

"I don't care how much it costs to file this lawsuit. I don't give a damn whether I make any money or lose a shitload of money. I'm going to sue these scumbags and show them that they can't get away with this crap… not around me and not around my darling Deidre."

CHAPTER 10

George DeRosa And Ann Schiller Discuss Libel Law

The tall willowy blond smiled, rising gracefully to greet the imposing, bearded lawyer marching towards her.

"George, it's wonderful to see you again. It's been far too long."

"It's lovely to see you too, Ann," replied George De Rosa as he sat in his usual seat at One Main Street Bar and Grille. "However, I suspect I know the reason for your kind invitation to lunch."

Ann ignored George's skeptical smirk.

"Aunt Amanda is very grateful for your legal advice which protected her when she was questioned by the police about the disappearance of Deidre's diamond ring. However, she's perplexed that you won't represent her in a libel suit against those posters who've made crazy accusations against her online. She's anxious to put the record straight by publicly taking a stand against these accusations. She's eager to file a lawsuit like the one just filed by Harold Brewster."

George nodded his head in sympathy.

"Ann, I'm very fond of your aunt Amanda. I completely understand why she's upset with the lies circulating on social media about her and her close friends. However, as we both know, libel cases are notoriously difficult to win here. It's a very different story in England, Amanda's former home."

"A difficult case wouldn't deter *you*, George. You've taken some of the toughest cases around. What's really going on?"

"Ann, few people in this world are more libeled against than lawyers. If you read the popular press, we all have two horns and a forked tail. Have you ever noticed how few lawyers sue for libel when they've been besmirched by the press?"

"No, but I'll take your word for it," Ann acknowledged.

After ordering a glass of pinot, George continued. "Most lawyers know only too well that filing a libel lawsuit makes the original nasty statement a thousand times more visible and dangerous to their reputation. Most libelous statements are quickly forgotten. However, when someone prominent files a libel lawsuit the public remembers what the author wrote or said about the plaintiff whenever a court hearing comes around. In libel cases, there are usually several court hearings before the matter goes to trial. A libel case can drag on for *years*. Given the defenses available to defendants in libel lawsuits under the First Amendment, a plaintiff's reputation may *never* be exonerated in the eyes of the public."

After the waiter brought George's glass of pinot and took their lunch order, George continued.

"In my humble opinion, bringing a libel lawsuit is *not* the smartest way for Amanda to put the record straight. Instead, your aunt should keep a low profile until the cops have completed their investigation. After she's been fully exonerated, all the vicious, nasty statements on Sleuths Anonymous will be viewed for what they are …ignorant and stupid."

"But George, the California Statute of Limitations for Libel requires that Aunt Amanda file a lawsuit within a year. The cops' criminal investigation could take much longer."

"*True*," the lawyer replied. "But I believe your Aunt Amanda's chances to win a libel lawsuit range from zero to nil."

"Why's that?"

"Because, your Aunt is *the* poster child for the legal definition of 'public figure' under the ruling in *New York Times v. Sullivan* and subsequent case law. Amanda's been famous ever since she became a teenage supermodel. She's been constantly featured in the news attending society events with famous rock stars. She regularly invites her high profile entertainment friends to play at her vineyard fundraisers. There are few people *on this earth* more famous than your aunt."

George paused while Ann tried to remember the now-famous specifics of the US Supreme Court ruling.

"George, I have to admit that my recollection of *New York Times v. Sullivan* and other recent cases is a bit rusty. Explain why my aunt being a public figure makes such a huge difference."

George smiled. "Ann, I'm not surprised you don't remember the specifics. Like most of our legal brethren who've never tried a libel case, you remember this famous precedent but not the details. I've defended the press in a few libel cases. However even I had to hit the books about how current libel law applies to statements posted on social media."

George rummaged in his briefcase and removed a folder. After reviewing some notes, he turned to Ann.

"Here's the scoop: If Amanda files a libel lawsuit against the press, she can't merely argue that the statements were false. In fact, she can't even argue that the press was negligent. Instead, as 'a public figure' under *New York Times v. Sullivan* and subsequent case law, she must also prove that, at the time of publication, the press either *knew* that social media BS wasn't true or the press showed *a reckless disregard* about whether the social media BS was true or not. Since no one at this stage of the game actually knows *who* stole the ring, it may be impossible for Amanda to meet this higher burden of proof."

"What about a lawsuit against the people who posted the garbage on Sleuths Anonymous?"

"Good luck with that," George said sarcastically. "As a plaintiff's lawyer, I rarely file a lawsuit unless I know the defendant has the financial resources to pay a judgment. Since we don't know the identity of the jokesters who posted that vile nonsense about your aunt, we haven't a clue whether they're rich, poor, or something in between.

"And another thing that escapes attention is that, pursuant to recent appellate rulings, plaintiffs in California can only sue for libel over false *facts*…not stupid, outrageous speculative opinion. Most obnoxious social media comments about your aunt fall squarely within the definition of 'wild speculative opinion' over what they *think* happened to this diamond ring."

George took a sip of his wine. He could tell from Ann's expression that she was a bit confused by his commentary.

"Let me give you a couple of examples. Ah, yes: Green Carbuncle's theory," George said with heavy derision. "Green Carbuncle posted that Amanda could profit handsomely from stealing a valuable diamond ring because she moves in high society circles. That part is true, as we've discussed. That poster-jokester then jumped to the outrageous conclusion that because Amanda moves in high society circles, she *must* have stolen the ring to sell it to one of her rich friends. Obviously, that's complete nonsense."

"*Agreed*," Ann replied.

"Another example: Hound of Belvedere posted that Amanda could've stolen the ring to sell it to one of her many celebrity ex-boyfriends. Again, this is wild speculation along the lines of "I think this happened because Amanda Jones' history includes dating rock stars."

"One of my favorites is the posting by Hound of Belvedere that Amanda Jones stole the ring because she's a Brit and Brits have 'sticky fingers.' Your aunt and I had a good laugh about that one but she told me—in confidence—that some Brits have an 'Artful Dodger' fixation. They walk off with valuables just to see if they can get away with it."

"You're joking."

"No, I'm not. It's a cultural thing. Brits aren't as violent as many of us but love to play hide and seek with the cops for fun. Amanda confided that she doesn't trust a couple of her closest British friends. When they visit, she watches them like a hawk, even though they're extremely wealthy. She jokingly assured me that she doesn't have 'an Artful Dodger fixation.'"

"Thank God for that."

"We also concluded that it's patently—and statistically—ridiculous to accuse every Brit of 'sticky fingers.' "

George paused to look at his notes. "Ann, here's the important point. When one of our local TV stations reported what was being posted on social media, it cautioned its viewers that the posts were *mere speculation*, so the public wouldn't take these postings as gospel truth. This is important because recent California Court of Appeal decisions have ruled that, if these statements were *mere speculation,* the statements might be outside the 'libel' definition."

"George, for heaven's sake, why would any court decide that these postings *weren't* libelous? They seem libelous to me!"

"Ah …" replied George with a broad smile. "Because, in their infinite wisdom, the California Court of Appeal has come up with the "*reasonable reader*" test when analyzing the nonsense posted on social media.

"Oh, like the 'reasonable man' test in tort law."

"Correct! For posts on social media to be held libelous, the garbage on social media must include *facts* that would make *the reasonable reader* or reasonable viewer, take the outrageous posting seriously. Ranting and venting on the Internet isn't libelous if the reasonable reader would surmise that the author is merely letting off steam."

After a long pause, Ann spoke. "OK George, I understand there are serious legal obstacles to my aunt winning a libel case against the press. I also understand that she risks losing money if she sues a bunch of anonymous posters. But maybe she's OK with that. Maybe she wants to go on record as standing up for herself. Maybe she wants to take a stand on principle. What about taking her case under those circumstances?"

George gave Ann one of his broadest smiles.

"Ann, the moment any client starts talking about filing a lawsuit *on principle*, I run for the hills…and so should you. It *always* means that the client wants something the legal system can't provide. Usually these clients want revenge or they secretly fantasize about emerging from the courthouse in a blaze of glory. When that doesn't happen, the client becomes extremely upset with his or her lawyer."

He paused while the waiter served lunch. After the waiter left, George leaned over, speaking quietly.

"Although your partner, Bertrand Wainwright, will do his very best to win Harold Brewster's lawsuit, on a personal level he probably doesn't care if Harold loses his libel lawsuit and ends up hating your partner's guts. Your firm's attorney-client retainer agreement probably outlines all the pitfalls we've been discussing today. But Amanda and I are different; we go back a long way. I will not risk ruining my longtime friendship with your aunt by accepting and losing her libel case 'on principle.'"

"Fair enough," Ann acknowledged, smiling.

"And there's something else. Libel lawsuits are one of those rare occasions when the corporate bar and the plaintiffs' bar *switch sides*. As you know, we plaintiff lawyers usually *sue* the rich and powerful. Corporate law firms like yours *defend* the rich and powerful... but libel cases are different."

"How so?"

"Corporate law firms like yours represent the rich and powerful when they think they've been libeled. We plaintiff lawyers usually *defend* the press and public's right to free speech. In the past, I've represented several newspapers after they were sued for libel. As a proud, paid-up member of the ACLU, I could never bring a libel lawsuit against the press. It's against my religion."

Ann glanced away and smiled.

"George, what you really mean is that you wouldn't want to get on the wrong side of the press because they might stop flattering you in their columns as one of our city's prominent, boldfaced names."

George chuckled.

"That too!" he replied.

CHAPTER 11

Deke Little Visits Charlie Bartino

Charlie Bartino opened his front door with a huge grin on his weatherbeaten brown face.

"Hi Deke, thanks for driving up to Sonoma. Diane and I are really pleased to see you. I just hate going into the City. I'm a country boy through and through."

"I suppose I'm one of those city slickers who you disdain," Deke Little smiled, revealing deep facial crevices.

"No...not you! Others maybe...but not you," Charlie said with a smile.

Diane stood to greet the immaculately dressed lawyer with grey eyes, grey crewcut, and square jaw.

"It's good to see you, friend," she smiled. "Let me take your coat. Charlie will get you a drink and we'll sit outside on the patio."

"That'll be a treat coming from fogbound San Francisco," Deke replied as he put down his coat.

Charlie went to the kitchen to make drinks while Diane and Deke sat down on the Bartino's comfortable patio furniture outside.

Diane leaned over to speak quietly to the lawyer. "Deke, these nasty posts on Sleuths Anonymous really have upset Charlie. He's mad about the accusations made against him *and* his friends. I hope you can calm him down."

"I'll do my best. I can understand why he's mad. But I may not be able to give him the advice he wants."

"Who pays a lot of attention to that nonsense, anyway?" she added firmly.

"Diane, you're exactly right. Charlie's got to understand that no one with any sense pays attention to it."

Charlie returned with the drinks and sat next to Diane. "Have you had a chance to read the load of cow dung that's posted on social media?" He asked angrily.

"Yes, and because it's cow dung you should let it slide right into the dirt for now."

"Hey...I thought you were some kind of trial lawyer!" Charlie shouted angrily.

Deke looked at Charlie without saying a word. The lawyer's deadpan facial expression reminded Charlie that Deke had a history of winning lawsuits for Charlie and his family.

"Hey … I'm sorry. I forgot my manners," Charlie said sadly. "Oddly enough, I told Harold Brewster to mind his manners when he exploded with rage the night that darn ring disappeared. I apologize to you, my friend."

Deke chuckled, which broke the ice. "Charlie, you know I can take a joke, especially from you. I couldn't be your lawyer all these years if I was one of those stiff necked corporate lawyers like Harold Brewster's lawyer, Wainwright. I've driven up from San Francisco so that we can discuss a few things face-to-face you may not want to hear."

"OK, I'm listening." Charlie folded his arms, expecting bad news.

"First, I can't take your libel case because I already represent a TV station being sued by Harold Brewster. If you file your own libel lawsuit, you may want to sue the same station that's already one of my clients."

"Ah...that's unfortunate," Diane replied. Charlie looked disappointed.

"But before I refer you to another lawyer, I want to advise you as a personal friend that bringing a libel lawsuit might not be in your best interest. In fact, it might be a big waste of your valuable time and money"

"Go on," Charlie said with annoyance.

"First, any lawyer looking at your case will carefully analyze the statements about you posted on Sleuths Anonymous. He or she will quickly figure out that these postings contain some true facts. You *were* charged with insider trading a few years back. You *are* also a well-known collector of antique military hardware. As you probably know, truth is a defense in any libel lawsuit."

"Yeah, but what about the damn lies and insinuations that this means I stole the engagement ring? That's complete phooey. Surely you don't believe that's true!"

"Charlie, of course I don't believe you stole the ring. I agree with you that the accusations by Dancing Man and Twisted Lip are outrageous. Both are clearly ridiculous."

"Yep...and that's why I want to sue those bastards for making ridiculous, outrageous statements."

"And I don't blame you. However, the TV newscaster hit the nail on the head when he described—live to the viewers—that these posts as wild speculation."

"So what?"

"Here's the tricky part. The California Court of Appeal recently ruled that social media posts that come under the category of 'ranting and raving' or wildly speculative opinion may *not* be libelous."

"*What?*" Charlie yelled. "Those bastards slander me in this manner... and their posts aren't libelous?"

"The California Court of Appeal ruled in similar situations that a person may not have been libeled *if* a reasonable reader wouldn't take these posts seriously."

"Deke, are you feeling OK?" Diane asked quickly before Charlie exploded with rage "What you are saying makes no sense to us."

Deke took a deep breath. "I agree that these rulings don't make sense to the average person in the street...or the average lawyer for that matter. However, current California case law states that Charlie may not be able to state a claim for libel if *the reasonable reader* wouldn't take the outrageous statements about him posted on Sleuths Anonymous seriously. The court reasoned in similar situations that Charlie's reputation in the community won't have been damaged by wild and crazy speculative statements if a reasonable reader wouldn't take the posts seriously."

"Jeez," Charlie replied. He was stunned.

Diane thought quickly. "That means that the more outlandish and preposterous the garbage posted on social media, the less likely someone can win a libel lawsuit against the person posting the garbage?"

"Correct," Deke replied scornfully. After a long pause, Deke continued.

"Charlie, I agree with you that the social media posts accusing you of committing a very serious crime *should be* libel. Accusing someone of committing crime is normally libel *per se* under ancient common law principles. However, the courts are grappling with how our common law principles apply to the freewheeling chatter on the Internet.

"The libel case law is evolving. Right now, though, if the accusations against you and your friends are only wildly speculative opinion, unsupported by any facts that might sway a reasonable reader into believing the nonsense, these statements may not be libelous under the 'reasonable reader' test.

"So let's analyze these statements. In your case, it's extremely unlikely that any reasonable reader would take seriously the crazy accusation that you stole this ring because you're a collector of military hardware.

Deke paused to give Charlie and Diane time to digest this analysis.

"It's also extremely unlikely that any reasonable reader would believe the preposterous accusation that you stole a $50 million ring because the Feds *wrongly* suspected you of illegal insider trading a few years ago. Neither accusation makes any sense at all.

"Bottom line: since no reasonable reader would take these wild and crazy accusations seriously, under current California appellate case law, your chances of bringing a successful libel lawsuit are considerably diminished."

"*Jeez,*" Charlie said again shaking his head in disgust.

CHAPTER 12

Peter Smith Visits His Favorite City

A few days later, Peter Smith took the Vallejo ferry to San Francisco to consult with his lawyer, Jack Murphy. Unlike Charlie, Peter was delighted to have an excuse to visit San Francisco, a favorite stomping ground in his younger days. At the downtown office that Jack Murphy shared with others, Peter looked at the décor.

"Jack needs my help in redecorating his office," Peter thought as he took a seat in the foyer. *"This décor is terrible. Maybe I can trade some redecorating work for legal fees when I file my lawsuit against those morons who have nothing better to do than throw dirt at me and others."*

Jack Murphy, a young red-haired lawyer with a freckled face and blue eyes greeted his client. "Good to see you again, Peter. What's all this about some idiots writing crap about you online?" He asked after they were comfortably seated in Jack's office.

Peter showed Jack copies of the offending posts that mentioned his involvement in the insider trading case years earlier.

"Ah," Jack responded sadly. "There's a problem. Sleuths Anonymous is one of my clients."

"But I don't want to sue Sleuths Anonymous or any of their employees," replied Peter. "It's not their fault what those nutcases write on that platform."

"True. But I represent Sleuths Anonymous whenever it's subpoenaed for information about the *identity* of anonymous users on its platform. Sleuths Anonymous wants to protect its users' identities, whenever possible."

"Oh," Peter relied sadly. "I guess I need to find another lawyer."

"Peter, that's true and I strongly encourage you to seek other counsel. I can give you the names of several excellent lawyers that will be happy to meet with you to advise you on this matter. However, since you're in my office, I'd like to share what I've learned since representing platforms like Sleuths Anonymous."

"Sure, I'd like to hear it."

"If you were my client in this matter, I'd advise you to refrain from filing a libel lawsuit because it's doubtful that you'd prevail…given current case law in California."

Jack took several minutes to describe the same legal rulings that Deke had discussed with Charlie and Diane.

"The case law involving social media is still developing," Jack added. "However, the accusation that you stole this ring because you were found *not guilty* of illegal insider trading is clearly so ridiculous that it's laughable. According to recent California Court of Appeal decisions, these accusations may not amount to libel because no one is likely to take these ridiculous accusations seriously."

"God…I am so relieved."

"Really?" The young lawyer sat bolt upright in his chair. "I'm very surprised. Usually clients don't like being told they don't have a strong case."

"I never wanted to sue anyone," Peter admitted, staring at his lawyer. "I only came to see you because Charlie and Bob want me to support them by filing my own lawsuit. I didn't want to let my buddies down. However, I can't afford a ton of legal fees. After that illegal insider trading case, I'm scared to death of the courtroom. I'd rather not see the inside of one again unless I'm summoned to serve on a jury."

Jack smiled. "Peter, you're smart."

Peter became animated. "Instead of filing a lawsuit, I'd prefer that my friends keep poking fun at these idiots by posting their own ridiculous theories on Sleuths Anonymous. They've been funnier than heck."

"Tell me more," Jack smiled.

"One of my friends posting as The Crooked Woman wrote that every Sonoma resident *must* be guilty of stealing this ring because they all live in the city where the theft took place."

"Oh...*that's* highly logical," Jack replied with raised eyebrows and a smirk. "Keep going. I'm enjoying this."

"Another friend posting as Seven-Percent Solution agreed with The Crooked Woman adding that Tim and Lucy Newman and their guests were so busy crushing grapes that they obviously didn't notice *thousands* of Sonoma residents trooping into the back of the wine cellar looking for the ring."

Jack laughed out loud and gave his client a high five.

"Peter, you've made my day. Let me take you to lunch so that you can tell me more about these hilarious posts. I should read Sleuths Anonymous more often...just to get a good laugh."

CHAPTER 13

The Courthouse Pigeons Coach Sidney

Lucy and Tim left Sidney in a dog-friendly hotel on Nob Hill to consult with Lillian Johnson about filing a libel lawsuit. Sidney ran to the window after two pigeons landed on the sill.

"*Hi Sidney,*" Sebastian, the younger pigeon, tweeted. "*Our country cousins told us you might be coming to the City. How's things?*"

"*G'Day, Courthouse Pigeons!*" Sidney's said with a big smile. "*Great to see you. I'm much happier since the last time we met. My humans Tim and Lucy aren't waiting to be barbecued in court about trades in tech stocks. This time, they're onto a real winner.*"

"*Tell us more,*" said Basil, the older pigeon, as he fluffed his feathers with a clawed foot.

"*Some humans been anonymously posting vicious lies and rumors about Tim that are totally untrue. The press has published the rumors. Tim and Lucy are talking with their lawyer Lillian Johnson about bringing a libel lawsuit against the press and the anonymous writers who spread the malicious rumors.*"

Basil puffed out his chest. "*Not so fast, Sidney. Libel lawsuits are tricky. Many sue. Few prevail.*"

Sidney looked puzzled. "*How come? As a smart, four-legged Silicon Valley Bro, it seems to me that Tim and Lucy have a slam-dunk case.*"

Basil looked stern. "*Sidney, you may be a smart, four-legged Silicon Valley Bro who knows a lot about technology. But you're as dumb as a sparrow when you start speculating about libel law.*"

Sebastian cocked his head to one side to show sympathy. "*Sidney, our nation has something called the First Amendment, which allows everyone to express opinions without fear that they'll be thrown in jail because they've offended someone in government. I live in North Beach, a haven for controversial ideas. The humans in North Beach are famous for expressing their opinions about the rich and powerful. They couldn't speak their minds without our First Amendment."*

"Sebastian's right," added Basil. *"Prominent humans, like your Tim, have great difficulty winning libel lawsuits because the courts have ruled that they're 'public figures.' As public figures, they're held to a higher burden of proof."*

Sidney was puzzled. *"What's a burden of proof?"*

"Anyone who files a lawsuit has to meet a certain burden of proof...otherwise their lawsuits are thrown out," replied Basil. *"If you're rich and prominent enough to pay a lawyer to file a libel lawsuit, you're probably a 'public figure'. Public figures can't simply prove in court that the social media posts are untrue. A public figure also has to prove that the speaker or writer knew that the postings were untrue at the time of publication OR didn't give a damn whether the statements was true or false."*

"Yeah," Sebastian concurred. *"And if you sue the press or media over a matter of public interest, you may get slapped by California's Anti-SLAPP law. This law was passed to stop the rich and powerful bringing frivolous libel lawsuits to muzzle journalists and the free press."*

Sidney visualized human journalists forced to wear the terrible muzzles he'd seen in the dog park. The vision wasn't a happy one.

"I hate muzzles. I can understand journalists not wanting to be muzzled when they report the news," he replied. *"But what about the anonymous posters who wrote all those bad things about my humans, Lucy and Tim and their friends online? Can't my humans sue and find out who wrote that load of rubbish?"*

Basil looked judicial. *"Maybe. It all goes back to the founding of our nation, when the authors of the Federalist Papers wrote anonymously. Since that era, the US Supreme Court has allowed all authors to remain anonymous unless they write stuff that's clearly libelous. Anonymous authors who are merely rude, controversial, or insulting are allowed to remain anonymous. The social media* platforms where they post don't have to disclose their identities."

Sidney thought it over. *"Hmm. Do I have a right to free speech? Am I allowed to bark to express myself?"*

Sebastian and Basil looked at one another.

"Humans have passed laws that give wildlife rights similar to the humans' right to free speech under the First Amendment," Basil replied, bobbing his head from side to side in a self-satisfied, superior manner. *"We can tweet, screech, and hoot to our friends at all hours. The humans aren't allowed to harass or shoot us, even if we keep them awake at night."*

"However," Basil continued in a condescending, low voiced tweet, *"domestic animals like you Sidney live closer to humans. The laws are different for you. You're not allowed to bark if it annoys your human neighbors. If that happens, the police will come to your home and demand that your humans keep you quiet or you will be locked up. However, you are allowed to bark to warn your humans about criminal intruders."*

"Wildlife rules are so cool," Sebastian chimed in. *"Visitors to tourist places like Monterey often complain about dogs barking all night. But they're not dogs— they're sea lions! Sea lions are protected wildlife. There's nothing the police, visitors, or hotel staff can do about sea lions' noisy barking."*

Sidney started to worry. *"Sounds like a libel lawsuit is bad news for my humans. Do you have any advice on how I can herd them away from this lawsuit?"*

Basil thought for a moment. *"According to our Avian Network, the humans still haven't discovered who stole the diamond ring. Sidney, perhaps you can help the humans find the thief using your acute sheepdog nose and intelligence. Once the thief's identity is discovered, all those nasty rumors about your humans will disappear."*

Sidney started to wag his tiny tail. *"I detected a wild animal or bird was in the cellar the night the jewel disappeared. Officer Hawk from the Sonoma Avian Highway Patrol has offered to help me find this creature because it may have seen what happened that night. Can you also send a request to the other birds and wildlife in the Bay Area to keep their eyes open for the ring?"*

"If you give us a detailed description of the ring, we will be happy to help," replied Basil.

"*Good thinking, Sidney*," Sebastian replied with enthusiasm, hopping from one bird foot to the other. "*Using our Avian Network of hawks, owls, gulls, herons, crows, pelicans, and pigeons, we have the entire Bay wired. When we spread the word around about this missing ring, we'll also ask every bird and animal to help identify those humans who are posting those mean rumors and lies about your humans.*"

"*Sidney, let me tell you a secret. The humans don't know this ... but we pigeons can read human writing.*"

CHAPTER 14

The Mainstream Press vs. Harold Brewster

The lawyers rose like an ocean wave as Judge Victoria Chang took the bench. They sat after the judge put down her papers.

"Counsel, I have read your motion arguments carefully, all of which cover several important points of law. This morning, the court requests that you address the court on specific facts or points of law involving your client and not merely repeat other counsels' arguments.

"I will first ask counsel for CBA Broadcasting Corporation to address the court on why his client was engaged in activities protected by California's Anti-SLAPP statute."

A smartly dressed lawyer with piercing grey eyes marched to a lectern placed between the plaintiff and defendant counsel tables. After a brief glance at his notes he stood up straighter.

"Your Honor, I'm Deke Little, counsel for CBA Broadcasting Company," he said a deep voice. "In 1992, the California legislature passed the nation's first Anti-SLAPP statute. This statute was designed to protect my client and other members of the press from meritless libel lawsuits designed to chill the constitutional right to free speech.

"Specifically, this statue allows my client and other members of the press to bring a motion to dismiss a libel lawsuit *where the press is engaged in a protected activity* within the meaning of California's Anti-SLAPP statute, *and* the plaintiff is unable to show that he is likely to prevail in his lawsuit against the press.

The judge nodded affirmatively. "Thank you, counsel. The court is familiar with this legislation. Please focus your argument on why *your* client was engaged in a protected activity under this legislation."

"Certainly, Your Honor," Deke Little replied briefly bowing his head. "Last year, a famous and valuable diamond ring worth $50 million disappeared from a private home in Sonoma. After this ring disappeared, several amateur detectives posted theories on the website Sleuths Anonymous about who might have the motive and opportunity to steal this ring. In the course of broadcasting news and information regarding this disappearance, my client reported on the various theories that had been posted on Sleuths Anonymous regarding this ring's disappearance.

"Plaintiff Harold Brewster's complaint alleges that the posts on Sleuths Anonymous about him were false, libelous, and damaging to his reputation. Mr. Brewster's complaint also alleges that *my client* slandered him when my client informed the public about these social media posts in the course of reporting the disappearance of this valuable diamond ring on TV. The complaint also alleges my client libeled plaintiff when these posts were added to my client's website."

The judge motioned to counsel to pause.

"Counsel, I have read several references to Sleuths Anonymous in the motion papers filed with the court. Please describe this website for the court record."

"Certainly, Your Honor. This website is designed to be used by amateur 'sleuths' who wish to assist the police with ongoing criminal investigations. The users are encouraged to use pseudonyms from famous Sherlock Holmes stories when posting anonymously on the site – hence the name *Sleuths Anonymous*."

"Thank you, counsel, please proceed."

"My client, CBA Broadcasting Company, is here today to request that the court dismiss Mr. Brewster's libel and slander claims against it on the grounds that (1) my client was reporting on *a matter of public interest*, namely the disappearance of a $50 million diamond ring; *and* (2) the plaintiff is unlikely to prevail in his libel and slander lawsuit against my client."

Deke Little glanced briefly at his notes before continuing.

"At this stage, it's important to note that a matter of public interest under California's Anti-SLAPP statute is *not* confined to matters involving public affairs or public officials. It also includes matters *in which the public takes an interest*."

Deke Little paused again to ensure he had the court's attention.

"Understood, counsel. Please proceed."

"My client contends that the disappearance of the $50 million diamond ring in Sonoma is a matter of great public interest. As stated in numerous affidavits filed with this court, this valuable diamond ring includes a famous pink diamond gemstone known in collectors' circles as the *Violette Diamond* surrounded by twelve white diamonds. This diamond ring disappeared during a Crush party in Sonoma attended by well-known celebrities and high-profile Silicon Valley executives."

"Counsel, can you remind the court what you mean by the term 'Crush'?"

"Certainly, Your Honor," Deke Little replied. "Crush occurs when wine grapes are delivered to a winery or other winemaking facility and the grapes are crushed into liquid form using a destemming machine."

"Thank you, counsel. Please proceed."

"Due to the fame and value of the Violette Diamond *and* its disappearance during a Crush party attended by many celebrities, this ring's disappearance received a great deal of media attention from local, national, and international news outlets. Since its disappearance, more than one million people have searched Google about this ring. Therefore, my client contends that this diamond ring and its disappearance is clearly a matter of *great public interest* within the meaning of California's Anti-SLAPP statute. Therefore, my client was clearly engaged in a protected activity under California's Anti-SLAPP statute.

"Since my client was engaged in a protected activity, current case law cited by my office and others present here today states that this court *must* dismiss this libel lawsuit against my client *unless* plaintiff Harold Brewster can show that he is likely to prevail with respect to his libel claims against my client."

"Thank you, counsel. I will ask you to address the likelihood of the plaintiff prevailing *after* we have heard from plaintiff's counsel regarding whether your client was engaged in a protected activity within the meaning of the Anti-SLAPP statute."

Deke Little picked up his notes and left the lectern. Bertrand Wainwright took his place.

"Your Honor, I represent the plaintiff Harold Brewster," he said as he straightened his bow tie. "My client contends that the disappearance of his fiancée's diamond ring was *not initially* a matter of public interest within the meaning of the Anti-SLAPP statute. This diamond ring was only in the news for a very brief period of time after its disappearance. The public only took a greater interest in the diamond ring's disappearance *after* preposterous social media postings on Sleuths Anonymous falsely accused my client and others of committing this theft."

Bertrand Wainwright picked up his notes. "Your Honor, I would now like to read these false accusations of criminal conduct into the court record."

The judge nodded.

"Thank you, Your Honor. First, an anonymous poster using the pseudonym Purple Headed League alleged that my client, Harold Brewster, stole the diamond ring to file a fraudulent claim with his insurance company. Specifically, this poster alleged that my client conspired with his fiancée to steal the ring and to secretly keep the ring or sell it to one of Mr. Brewster's wealthy Silicon Valley friends.

"Another anonymous poster using the pseudonym Bohemian Dude agreed with Purple Headed League's outlandish post and alleged that the behavior of my client's fiancée was evidence that my client was guilty of insurance fraud. Both posts are clearly libelous because there's not a shred of evidence before this court that my client Harold Brewster or his fiancée, Deidre Langton, stole the ring."

Bertrand Wainwright paused to look down at his notes. He picked up a sheet of paper.

"Yet another anonymous poster using the pseudonym Swamp Adder alleged—and I quote—"I'm personally familiar with the career of this dishonest, narcissistic entrepreneur."This poster went on to allege that my client stole the diamond ring to give it to *a new love interest* whom this poster claimed to observe my client meeting at breakfast in Woodside.

"But Swamp Adder didn't stop there," Bertrand Wainwright added as his right hand picked up another sheet of paper. "This post also alleged, —and I quote "I and many others in Silicon Valley suspect that Harold Brewster faked the initial lab work and animal testing needed to obtain Fast Track FDA approval for his UTI vaccine. I and many others in Silicon Valley also suspect that Brewster faked his company's financials during the acquisition of his lucrative start-up by "big pharma." Faking lab tests and company financials is typical Brewster behavior.' "

The lawyer put down the second sheet of paper, shaking his head with contempt.

"Your Honor, this post is also clearly libelous because it alleges without a shred of evidence that my client is guilty of committing several crimes. In other words, he not only stole the ring as alleged by two other posters but also committed criminal fraud with respect to corporate financial statements and information submitted to the FDA."

The judge raised her hand to signal that the lawyer should pause. "The court understands that it's counsel's position that the posts on Sleuths Anonymous are libelous. However, the court requests that counsel address the specific issue of whether *the mainstream press* represented in court today were engaged in a protected activity within the meaning of California's Anti-SLAPP statute."

"Certainly, Your Honor. The mainstream press represented here today *republished every libelous social media allegation against my client.* Had this not occurred, the small amount of interest generated shortly after the diamond ring disappeared would have died down. The general public only took a much greater interest in the diamond ring's disappearance *after* the mainstream press libeled my client by focusing enormous and unwarranted attention on the false accusations posted on social media about my client.

"In their motion papers, several counsel representing the mainstream press argue that their clients' activities were not libelous because they only *republished* the false and libelous accusations that my client was guilty of criminal behavior. However, the law is clear. Libel is libel—even when it is *republished.*"

Bertrand Wainwright took his seat. After listening to arguments from other defense counsel, the judge looked at the courtroom clock and adjourned the morning hearing.

"Counsel, we will now take a lunch break until 1:30 this afternoon. After the court reconvenes, I will hear argument regarding whether plaintiff Harold Brewster is likely to prevail in his libel lawsuit against the members of the mainstream press represented in court today."

CHAPTER 15

The Courthouse Pigeons Report
To The Avian Network

"The right of free speech is under attack. The human press is fighting back," tweeted the pigeons, seagulls, herons, pelicans, and crows as they swooped down to give Bay Area domestic and wild animals the latest news.

"The courthouse pigeons report that a huge courtroom battle is taking place in the San Francisco Superior Court. Lawyers representing television, radio, and print media demand that the court throw out Harold Brewster's libel lawsuit. We'll bring you the latest scoop once we get it. Stay tuned for the future developments."

Outside the building, the courthouse pigeons gathered to brief the Avian Network about the current state of play in the courtroom. Basil, the most senior courthouse pigeon, puffed out his chest.

"Humans use an inferior version of our Avian Network known as 'social media' to distribute information. The courtroom proceedings today arise from damning accusations on social media that the plaintiff, Harold Brewster, stole his fiancée's valuable $50 million diamond ring.

"This ring mysteriously disappeared from the Sonoma home of our friend, Sidney Newman, a domestic sheepdog. In the courtroom this morning lawyers representing television, radio, and newspapers are standing up for their right to keep the human public informed on what is posted on social media—even if these social media posts are libelous."

"Things are heating up," Sebastian, a young hipster courthouse pigeon, tweeted as he hopped from one foot to another. *"Plaintiff Harold Brewster looked mad as hell when he left the courthouse during the lunch break. He complained loudly to his lawyer Bertrand Wainwright that the court hearing was taking too long. The judge should have already ruled in his favor. He also*

complained that his time is 'way too valuable' to attend court all day. We courthouse pigeons frequently hear these complaints from 'techie' humans. If Brewster's time is too valuable to attend court, maybe he shouldn't have filed his lawsuit in the first place."

"Clearly the plaintiff has unrealistic expectations," the more solemn Basil replied. "Courtroom proceedings always take longer than the humans expect. This reminds me of the occasion when our friend, Sidney Newman, thought his humans, Lucy and Tim Newman had a 'slam dunk' libel case. We courthouse pigeons educated Sidney about the complexities of libel law. Fortunately for Sidney, the Newmans' attorney Lillian Johnston advised Lucy and Tim Newman against filing a lawsuit until the authorities have completed their investigation into the diamond ring's disappearance. Having his humans involved in a libel lawsuit would have made our friend Sidney's home life very stressful."

"Yeah," replied Sebastian, nodding his pigeon head. "Harold Brewster probably didn't listen to his lawyer's advice that libel lawsuits are difficult to win. High-powered techie humans always think that the law can be bent to reflect their opinions. We courthouse pigeons know different."

"During Mr. Brewster's lunchtime vent, his lawyer's expression looked non-committal," Basil added. "Counsellor Wainwright wasn't giving anything away... even to us courthouse pigeons. Deke Little and the other defense lawyers representing the press looked quietly confident when they exited the courthouse during the lunch break. From our observations of these lawyers and Mr. Brewster's undignified behavior, it would appear that the hearing isn't going particularly well for Mr. Brewster."

"Yeah...and it'll be another exciting courtroom hearing this afternoon," Sebastian chirped, nodding his iridescent head and neck. "We'll carefully watch the lawyers and their clients when they arrive and leave the courthouse. We'll listen in on their conversation and report back to the Avian Network and its affiliates."

"Stay tuned for the latest developments!"

CHAPTER 16

The Courtroom Battle Resumes

"The court is now in session," the court bailiff's voice boomed as Judge Victoria Chang took the bench. After the judge placed papers on her elevated desk she instructed the two lawyers.

"Counsel, as I indicated earlier, the court will now hear argument regarding the second legal issue before the court. This issue is whether plaintiff Harold Brewster is *likely to prevail* in his libel lawsuit against the members of the mainstream press represented in court today. I will first call on counsel for CBA Broadcasting to address the court about this issue."

Deke Little walked to the lectern. "Your Honor, my client CBA Broadcasting contends that plaintiff Harold Brewster is very unlikely to prevail in his libel lawsuit against my client because he is a public figure. As such, he's required to meet a higher burden of proof pursuant to *New York Times v. Sullivan* and subsequent court precedent regarding public figures."

"Counsel, let me interrupt you for a second. Why should the court find that plaintiff Harold Brewster is a public figure requiring him to meet this higher burden of proof?"

"Plaintiff Harold Brewster is a public figure because his career has attracted a large amount of media attention resulting from the enormous success of his biotech start-up Vakzine4U. He's been featured in numerous national and international technology and biotechnology publications. He has attended many high-profile events, such as the annual World Economic Forum in Cologny, Switzerland. Before the acquisition of his company by Mammuthus Pharmaceuticals he was listed in the article *Top*

Young CEOs to Watch. In Silicon Valley and other technology circles, Mr. Brewster is a household name."

"Thank you, counsel. Please proceed."

"In addition to plaintiff's high profile, his purchase of the famous Violette Diamond ring worth $50 million at a public auction in London also generated a large amount of publicity. He may not be the first Silicon Valley executive to buy a famous, valuable piece of jewelry. However, he was one of the first to *bid* on a famous, valuable piece of jewelry at a London public auction that attracted agents representing the rich and famous globally.

"As many of us argued this morning, the disappearance of this valuable diamond ring from the Newman home in Sonoma generated local, national, and international press. If the court finds that plaintiff has not acquired the level of pervasive fame that makes him a public figure for all purposes, plaintiff is at the very least a public figure for the limited purpose of matters pertaining to the disappearance of the $50 million diamond ring."

"Thank you, counsel. Please continue."

"Thank you, Your Honor. Pursuant to *New York Times v. Sullivan* and subsequent case law, a public figure like Mr. Brewster must prove in court that my client *acted with malice* when it reported the social media debate taking place on Sleuths Anonymous. This doesn't require plaintiff to prove that my client acted maliciously, as that term is commonly used. However, current case law does require that a public figure such as Mr. Brewster must prove that my client either *knew that the facts were false* when it republished them or showed a *reckless disregard* as to whether the facts were true or false"

"Counsel, I appreciate your reference to this famous precedent of which the court is well aware. Please address the court on what relevance, if any, this case precedent has on writings posted on social media."

Deke Little bowed his head.

"Thank you, Your Honor. I was just coming to that important issue. According to recent California Court of Appeal decisions cited in the motion papers before the court, *opinions alone* posted on social media— however foolhardy or wrong—are insufficient to form the basis of a libel lawsuit. To support a libel lawsuit against my client and other members of the press represented here today, the plaintiff must prove that my client knew that the *facts* in the social media posts were untrue or that my client showed reckless disregard about whether the *facts* were true or false.

"The evidence before the court is that my client kept the public informed about the heated debate taking place online regarding the disappearance of the $50 million diamond ring. However, most of this debate concerned theories, suspicions, and opinions—not *facts* as required by the California Court of Appeal.

"Thank you, counsel. Do you have anything else to add?"

"Yes, Your Honor. It is also important to note that my client *never endorsed* any of the theories, suspicions, or opinions posted on Sleuths Anonymous about the plaintiff. To the contrary, throughout my client's reporting about the disappearance of this valuable diamond ring, my client's journalists voiced great skepticism about the theories and opinions posted on Sleuths Anonymous alleging criminal conduct by the plaintiff and others present at the Crush party where the diamond ring disappeared.

"After contacting the plaintiff for his response to these posts, my client also published plaintiff's denial that he had engaged in any criminal conduct.

"The evidence before the court is that my client reported what was happening in social media in a *fair and accurate manner.* This evidence is completely at odds with *any* claim by Mr. Brewster that that my client's journalists acted with malice against the plaintiff as required by *New York Times v. Sullivan* and subsequent case law.

"Since it is extremely *unlikely* that plaintiff will prevail in his libel lawsuit against my client, my client respectfully requests the court grant this motion to dismiss so that my client CBA Broadcasting can continue to keep the public informed of matters of public interest without fear of retribution by someone as rich and powerful as Mr. Brewster."

After Deke Little took his seat, Bertrand Wainwright rose to address the court.

"Your Honor, my client Harold Brewster is *not* a public figure under *New York Times v. Sullivan* and subsequent case law or for any purpose related to California's Anti-SLAPP legislation. He may be well known in certain "geeky" technology circles. However, he has never acquired the type of pervasive fame of a movie star, sports star, television personality, or politician that would make him a public figure for all purposes."

"Counsel, what about defense counsel's argument that Harold is a public figure for the limited purpose of the matters pertaining to the disappearance of the diamond ring?"

"Your Honor, in the line of cases where private individuals were found by the courts to have become public figures for a limited purpose, those individuals injected themselves into the public arena with regards to a matter of public interest. This case is clearly distinguishable from those cases. My client never injected himself into the public arena regarding the disappearance of this valuable diamond ring. To the contrary, my client Harold Brewster and his fiancée have gone out of their way to avoid press coverage regarding this matter."

"OK, counsel, please proceed."

"As I argued this morning, the diamond ring's disappearance initially generated a small amount of press coverage. It was briefly covered by local, national, and international news…but only for a day or so. The public did not take great interest in the ring's disappearance until posts on Sleuths Anonymous made false accusations that my client had engaged in criminal conduct."

"Under our common law principles, allegations that a person engaged in criminal conduct are *libel per se*. The press republished every single *libel per se* accusation posted on Sleuths Anonymous involving my client. Before this occurred, my client was never a public figure for any purpose. Therefore, my client shouldn't be required to meet the higher burden of proof required by *New York Times v. Sullivan*. Instead my client should only be required to show a likelihood that the defendants were *negligent as to the truth* when they republished the lies and distortions about my client posted on social media.

The judge raised her hand.

"Counsel, if the court finds that the plaintiff is either a public figure for all purposes or for the limited purpose of matters pertaining to the disappearance of the diamond ring, can your client meet the higher standard required of public figures cited by defense counsel."

"Most certainly, Your Honor. The evidence before the court shows that the mainstream press represented here in court today acted as if they didn't care a jot whether the social media posts were true or false. In other words, even if they claim that they didn't *know* the posts were untrue at the time of publication, the press most certainly *acted in reckless disregard* as to whether these posts were true or false."

"All right, counsel. But what about defense counsel's argument that the posts on social media were only theories or opinions?"

"Your Honor, some of the posts were indeed couched as theories and opinions." Bertrand Wainwright acknowledged as his client glared at him. "However, these theories and opinions were also supported by spurious facts. For example, one poster alleged that my client's fiancée acted suspiciously. Another alleged that my client had faked lab tests and company financials. These are all *facts* that support the spurious opinions posted on social media."

"Counsel, what about the defense counsel's argument that the press reported on the social media postings in a fair and accurate manner?"

"Your Honor, when counselor Deke Little argues before this court that the press acted in a fair and accurate manner, he is presumably raising the defense of Neutral Reportage, which has been upheld by some states as a defense in a libel lawsuit. However, to date, our California courts and legislature haven't adopted this Neutral Reportage defense. Even if the court rules that Neutral Reportage should apply in this case, my client contends that the press coverage was anything but fair and accurate.

"The evidence before the court is that the press republished all of the outrageous accusations of criminal conduct posted on social media about my client, probably as a way to improve ratings and circulation. As a result, these outrageous accusations acquired more credibility with the public—and therefore became much more damaging—than if the mainstream press had simply ignored them.

"Plaintiff respectfully submits that he will prevail in his libel *per se* claims against the mainstream press, even if the court rules that he must meet the higher burden of proof required of a public figure pursuant to *New York Times v. Sullivan* and subsequent case law.

"Since the evidence shows that my client Harold Brewster will prove at trial that he was libeled *per se* on social media *and* by certain members of the mainstream press, my client contends that the court should not dismiss this case against any member of the mainstream press before this case comes to trial."

CHAPTER 17

The Judge's Decision

Harold Brewster glared at his lawyer as they both sat with Phil Taylor in a Palo Alto conference room at Horace & Fitzgerald.

"A friend called me this morning to say that he'd heard on the news that Judge Chang has dismissed my libel lawsuit against the mainstream press. What the heck does she think she's doing and what the hell does it mean?"

Bertrand Wainwright cleared his throat. "Unfortunately, Mr. Brewster, the judge agreed with opposing counsel's argument that the press was engaged in a protected activity within the meaning of California's Anti-SLAPP statute because it was reporting on a matter of public interest.

"She also ruled that you were unlikely to prevail in your libel lawsuit against the press, given the myriad defenses available to the press based on the nation's First Amendment. The most hopeful part of the ruling from your standpoint is that she also ruled the media reported on a matter of public interest *in a fair and accurate manner.* As I argued before the court, this test has never been applied by our California Courts. It's unsettled law and may be vulnerable to attack on appeal."

"Yeah...you and your fancy argument. It didn't exactly produce a good result, did it?" Harold sneered.

A long painful silence ensued. Phil Taylor was the first to speak.

"So, Bertrand, where does this leave the case?" He asked quietly.

"Unfortunately, it means that, unless we file an appeal of the judge's ruling within the requisite time period, Mr. Brewster' claims against the mainstream press are dead."

"And...?"

"It also means that pursuant to the California's Anti-SLAPP statute Mr. Brewster must pay all legal fees incurred by the mainstream press in fighting his lawsuit to date."

"I f---g don't believe it," Harold yelled. "I hired you guys to bring a lawsuit that would stop the press humiliating me and Deidre. Now you say I pay the legal fees of the damned idiots who humiliated us?"

"Mr. Brewster, that the judge's decision," Bertrand Wainwright. "Clearly we don't agree with this decision, but…"

"Oh, *you don't agree with this decision*," Harold's voice sniped back at his lawyer. "Well what are you going to do about it? Do you really expect me to pay the exorbitant cost of an appeal so that you can jack up your fees remedying your own colossal loss in court? You must think I'm some kind of idiot."

"I think we've come to a point where this law firm can no longer represent you in this matter," Bertrand Wainwright replied, lowering his voice and speaking sternly. "I will inform the court that lawyer and client have irreconcilable differences. I will request that the court postpone the Sleuths Anonymous motion to quash your subpoena seeking the identities of all the anonymous posters who wrote about you on that platform. A postponement will give you time to find new counsel."

Bertrand Wainwright stood up, replaced his laptop in his briefcase, and walked towards the door. He paused, turned to his client. "Good day to you sir," he said before leaving the conference room.

CHAPTER 18

The Avian Network Visits Sidney

A tiny songbird flew to Sidney's side as he snoozed on the patio of the Newman home in Sonoma.

"Wake up, Sidney. I have news from the courthouse pigeons."

Sidney immediately sat up. *"Don't worry, songbird. I never sleep when I'm on duty. I always have one eye open. What's going on?"*

"Judge Victoria Chang dismissed Harold Brewster's libel lawsuit against the press! The newspapers and television stations are trumpeting the judge's ruling as a huge victory for free speech and freedom of the press."

"Oh dear. This ruling will make Harold as difficult to live with as a hungry crocodile," Sidney replied as he paced up and down the patio.

"And that's not all," the songbird sang sadly. *"Apparently, Mr. Brewster must pay all legal fees incurred by the press in fighting his lawsuit. The courthouse pigeons think that these legal fees may total thousands of dollars."*

"Oh, no!" Sidney replied as he thought about Deidre and her lost ring. *"This is terrible news. Poor Deidre. She's such a sweet Sheila. I hope Harold doesn't take this loss out on her."*

"The courthouse pigeons also said to tell you that you should feel very lucky that your humans didn't file a similar lawsuit."

Sidney groaned deeply. He was relieved that Lucy and Tim hadn't also sued the press for libel. However, he was annoyed at the patronizing superiority of the courthouse pigeons. He didn't blame Sebastian…but he found Basil insufferable at times.

"Sounds like the law is an ass," growled Sidney. *"It's stupidly rewarding bad behavior by the press. Do our brilliant courthouse pigeons have any words of wisdom about what happens next?"* Sidney tried to keep the sarcasm out

of his voice. He knew it wasn't the songbird's fault that things had gone badly for Harold Brewster at the courthouse.

"*The courthouse pigeons report that Harold's libel lawsuit can still proceed against the anonymous posters on Sleuths Anonymous. Trouble is…no one knows who they are.*" The songbird reprised her sad song.

An elegant green heron joined Sidney and the songbird. "*Heard the news?*" She asked as she turned her graceful neck to preen her lovely feathers.

"*Yeah…and I feel sorry for Deidre,*" whimpered Sidney. "*Everyone forgets that it was Deidre's ring that disappeared. She hasn't accused anyone of anything. She hasn't filed a lawsuit against anyone, even though some hooligans posted rubbish about her on Sleuths Anonymous.*"

After a long pause, Sidney sighed with exasperation. "*Why can't any of you birds bring me some good news? I'm surprised that none of you spotted anything that might tell me what happened the night Deidre's ring disappeared. We animals and birds pride ourselves on being smarter than the humans but we aren't covering ourselves with glory on this one.*"

"Hmmm, I agree," replied the green heron. "*Let me check with Officer Hawk to see if he's learned anything new. Trouble is, if he'd learned something, he'd probably have told us by now.*"

"*Maybe he's keeping the information close to his breast,*" replied the songbird hopefully. "*These bird cops usually don't squawk until they've wrapped up their investigation.*"

"*He was supposed to try find the mysterious creature in the wine cellar around the time the ring disappeared,*" growled Sidney. "*There's nothing confidential about that.*"

"*OK, Sidney, we'll find Officer Hawk and ask him to let you know of any progress on that front,*" replied the green heron. The songbird nodded enthusiastically.

Sidney stopped sulking. He suddenly thought how the birds were taking time away from foraging food for their survival to bring him news from the Avian Network. As a comfortable domestic sheepdog, he never faced death by starvation.

"Thank you, mates for taking time away from your busy schedules to bring me this news," Sidney replied. *"When I get back to Palo Alto, I'll also ask the Peninsula Avian Network whether they've discovered who wrote the social media posts."*

He paused for a moment.

"In truth, I'm not fond of Harold. He's arrogant, even by techie mogul standards. The night the ring disappeared, he behaved like a yobbo towards everyone…even Deidre. However, these anonymous posters also accused darling Deidre of involvement in a criminal conspiracy. Another accused Harold of having an affair with another woman! These posts must have hurt Deidre deeply.

"We must find out who wrote this stinking bilge."

CHAPTER 19

Enter Kimberly Hayward

Ann Schiller sat in the San Francisco lobby of The Law Offices of Kimberly Hayward waiting for Kimberly to join her. The two lawyers had been close friends since the days they worked at the prestigious white-shoe law firm, Hampton & Elliot, before its demise.

Ann marveled at Kimberly's pluck in turning down invitations by several large law firms in San Francisco to join their partnership ranks. Ann's partners at Horace & Fitzpatrick suggested Ann recruit Kimberly to join their litigation department. Ann had tried—to no avail.

"Hi, Ann! Great to see you." The auburn-haired Kimberly greeted Ann as she entered the lobby. "I hope you're not headhunting again." Ann smiled but didn't reply as they walked to the nearby conference room. "Even if you are, I'm still delighted to see you. It's been a while since we fought that insider trading case for the group your British aunt called *The Sonoma Five*," Kimberly added as they took their seats.

"And it's something similar that has brought me to your office again," replied Ann.

"Oh no...not *another* insider trading case?"

"No. This time I'm on a more delicate mission and it's very confidential. A client of our firm, Harold Brewster, has managed to get into a huge fight with one of my partners, Bertrand Wainwright. Bertrand is representing Harold Brewster in a libel lawsuit. Have you read anything about this case? It's been splashed all over the newspapers and TV reports."

"Of course. Whenever the press is sued for libel by a rich person like Harold Brewster, they trumpet their First Amendment rights all over the media. The libel suit is about scurrilous posts on social media claiming that Harold Brewster and his fiancée stole their own $50 million ring, correct?"

"Correct."

"Hmm, Wainwright's considered our local expert on libel law. Most lawyers in the Bay Area consult him if they have a client itching to file a libel lawsuit. A few years back, a corporate client came into my office wanting to sue for trade libel after some idiot had written something stupid on social media. Bertrand was very helpful when I sounded him out on the case. If anyone can win a libel lawsuit for your client, it's Bertrand Wainwright."

Ann nodded. "Kimberly, unfortunately, Harold Brewster's libel lawsuit has taken a turn for the worse. Judge Victoria Chang recently dismissed all of Harold Brewster's claims against the TV stations and newspapers that covered the social media posts. The judge's decision cited the Anti-SLAPP Act and a Neutral Reportage defense. Have you heard of this Neutral Reportage defense?

"Nope, but most of my clients don't usually seek my advice because they've been libeled. They have more serious legal problems, such as trouble with the criminal justice system."

"Me too. However, I've recently researched the Anti-SLAPP Act. It was passed to prevent libel lawsuits from stifling free expression on the Internet. As you probably know, Neutral Reportage gives the press a quick and easy dismissal...*if* the press shows that the news reports covered a matter of public interest and the reporting was neutral and unbiased. Once the judge decided to apply this defense, my partner Bertrand was unable to convince the judge that Harold Brewster was likely to win his libel lawsuit against the mainstream press."

"Sounds as if Brewster and your partner were unlucky with judge selection. But we all know that libel lawsuits are notoriously difficult. Everyone's right not to be libeled slams up against our First Amendment protecting everyone's right to free speech and the freedom of the press.

The latter are sacrosanct in this country."

"True. But the judge also ruled that Harold Brewster has to pay the attorneys' fees of the members of press recently dismissed from his lawsuit. As you can imagine, Harold got extremely angry and took it out on his attorney. Bertrand has filed a motion for our firm to withdraw on the usual grounds of irreconcilable differences between lawyer and client."

"Nice guy. Nice client. But what do you want me to do about it?"

"Meet with Harold Brewster to see if you would be willing to take on his case."

Kimberly stared at Ann. "*What?* You've got to be kidding. If Bertrand Wainwright can't win, why do you think I'd get a better result? Besides this Harold Brewster sounds like a piece of work. Ann, one of the advantages of having my own law firm is that I don't need to represent every jerk that has the resources to pay the firm's legal fees."

Ann looked down at the table. "Kimberly, I understand your hesitation but please hear me out. Bertrand's motion to withdraw will be heard next week. Once this motion is granted, Harold will be left fighting his libel case without counsel."

"Ann, why are you concerned about that? Happens every day. Unreasonable people make unreasonable demands of the legal system. When they don't get what they want in court, they either fail to pay their lawyer or their lawyer quits fighting Mission Impossible. Sounds as if Harold Brewster deserves what's coming to him."

"Kimberly, my aunt Amanda and my friend Lucy Newman are both concerned about Harold's fiancée, Deidre. She's a sweetheart. Salt of the earth. When she moved in with rich techie Harold, she didn't have to work. However, she continued to teach at the local public school in San Carlos because she loves teaching.

"Harold needs a good lawyer to represent him. Frankly, I thought of you because any new lawyer taking this case needs to be strong enough to manage Harold, so that he doesn't take his setbacks in court out on his lawyer ... or Deidre."

"Ann, I understand that your aunt and Lucy Newman may be very concerned about Deidre. However, you're not the emotional type who's easily swayed by kith and kin. You're a former federal prosecutor, for heaven's sake. Something else is going on. My hunch is that you are seriously worried about a miscarriage of justice taking place. Am I right?"

"Yes," Ann nodded her head sadly. "I don't think that either Harold or Deidre stole this $50 million ring...but the crazy posts on social media are making their lives hell. The same nonsense happened to my aunt. Fortunately, the crazy allegations against my aunt died down. However, she hates the mean BS that's posted online...and so do I. If Harold Brewster can discover the identity of the anonymous posters, Harold and Deidre might be able to find out who's posting this crazy stuff against them. Without a lawyer, Harold's dead in the water."

"OK, Ann," Kimberly said with a sigh. "Tell me where the case stands."

"As I mentioned, Judge Chang cited the Neutral Reportage defense used in other jurisdictions to dismiss claims against the press."

"What's so controversial about that? Sounds reasonable to me, especially if the plaintiff is deemed a public figure."

"Our California Supreme Court has spoken favorably about this defense in the past. However, neither the California Court of Appeal or the California Supreme Court have *applied* this defense in a California libel case to date. In other words, the judge is making new law for this jurisdiction. Harold may have a passing shot at having the judge's decision overturned on appeal."

"Hmm, sounds a long shot."

"Correct. However, if he can keep his lawsuit alive, it will give him and his lawyer more time to track down the identities of the anonymous posters."

"And where does that part of the case stand?"

"Wainwright served a subpoena on Sleuths Anonymous seeking

information about the identities the anonymous posters. Sleuths Anonymous has filed a motion to quash this subpoena. A hearing date has been set. Wainwright filed a request to continue this motion until his request to be removed from the case is heard and Harold has the opportunity to find new counsel."

"Oh...great," Kimberly didn't hide her sarcasm. "All the signals are out that Harold's case is falling apart. Out of interest, who's the principal lawyer on the other side?"

Ann smiled. "I was getting to that. My husband, Jack Murphy. is representing Sleuths Anonymous"

Kimberly laughed. "You've got to be kidding me."

"No, I'm not kidding. Jack strongly believes in fighting to protect the right to free speech under the First Amendment. He thinks this is more important than unmasking social media posters who are writing garbage. He knows that I don't agree with this position. I don't think that anonymous posters should always be allowed to remain anonymous."

"Sounds like a tough legal argument is taking place inside your home," Kimberly teased.

Ann laughed. "Yes, but you know our personal histories. We don't let our differences of opinion about the law ruin our relationship."

Kimberly looked at Ann. "You and Jack always remind me of Robin Hood and Maid Marion. Jack's the modern-day Robin Hood fighting in court to steal from the rich and powerful to give to the poor. You're Maid Marion, the Norman princess representing the same rich and powerful who falls in love with Robin."

Both lawyers smiled at Kimberly's analogy.

"Well, Ann, once again you've caught me at a good moment. I've plenty of time on my hands now that my marriage has fallen apart."

"What? Oh, no!"

"Oh, yes," Kimberly replied bitterly. "Last week my husband informed me that he's fallen in love with someone at work. Throughout our marriage, he complained about the amount of time I spend at the office. I always joked that the law is a jealous mistress. The joke's now on me."

After a long pause Kimberly continued. "Again, purely out of interest, who are the other characters in the cast that are involved in this lawsuit?"

"Deke Little represented the principal defendant, CBA Broadcasting, in the recent motion to dismiss. You'll be up against Deke if you take on the appeal."

Kimberly's gloomy expression faded. Her sense of humor returned.

"Talking about the Robin Hood legend, Deke's my idea of a modern-day Little John. He's wealthy, debonair, and always dresses immaculately. But, lurking in the background, there's a rugged tough guy you wouldn't want to come across in a dark area of Sherwood Forest."

Kimberly grinned mischievously. "I've always found Deke rather attractive, like the anti-hero in a classic Hollywood movie."

Ann laughed. "Really?"

"Yes...really. But speaking of our former colleagues in the insider trading case, is George De Rosa involved?"

"George represented my aunt during the police interviews about the missing diamond ring. However, he refused to take her libel lawsuit. He said it was against his religion to sue the press."

"I can believe that...knowing George's close relationship with the press. He's never out of the media spotlight. Did your aunt file a lawsuit?"

"Fortunately, no. She and her close friend Lady Roberta decided they'd 'rise above it, darling,'"

Kimberly smiled at Ann's mimicry of her aunt's English accent.

"OK, Ann, for your sake I'll meet with Harold Brewster after I've researched the latest developments in libel law and social media. However, I won't represent Mr. Brewster unless I think I can do something with his case. Before I take him on, I'll need to make him listen. This won't be easy if Brewster suffers from the Silicon Valley disease 'I'm always right and I'll always win.'"

After both women rose from the table, Kimberly looked at Ann with a raised eyebrow. "That said, I'd be delighted to oppose Jack and Deke in this case.

"We can't let have Jack and Deke have it *all* their own way, can we, Ann?" She added a conspiratorial wink as the meeting ended.

CHAPTER 20

Kimberly Hayward Meets Harold Brewster

"Hi, I'm Kimberly Hayward. It's good of you to come into San Francisco to meet with me today."

Kimberly took a seat at the conference table opposite a dark-haired man with a long rectangular beard, a current fashion among techies.

"It's good of you to meet with me," Harold Brewster mumbled as he rose to shake Kimberly's hand. They were barely seated when he burst out, "I suppose you already know that I've lost my lawsuit against the press. My lawyer's given up on me. From what I can tell, it won't be long before I totally lose the lawsuit."

Looking at Harold's frightened eyes, Kimberly began to feel sorry for him. He was clearly impetuous and hot tempered. However, he didn't appear to be the smug smartass she'd envisioned after her earlier conversation with Ann. Instead, he had an endearing naïve quality that appealed to the battle-hardened trial lawyer.

"Yes, I've reviewed your lawsuit," Kimberly replied slowly. "I've read the vicious posts on Sleuths Anonymous. I can well understand why you and your fiancée are furious. I've also read the judge's recent ruling. You're right. You've suffered a serious setback in your lawsuit against the mainstream press. However, before we get into the details, I'd like to hear from you what you're hoping to achieve from this lawsuit."

"Good question!" Harold replied as he ran his hands through his hair in exasperation. "When I hired Bertrand Wainwright, I was hoping to punish all those people who'd made Deidre's life—and mine—hell with their filthy lies. I now feel *I'm* the one who's being punished by filing this lawsuit."

"After what you've been through, I'm not surprised. But…and this is important…do you fully understand what you're up against in terms of the law governing libel lawsuits?"

"The First Amendment right to free speech."

"Correct. Anything else?"

"God, isn't that enough?" Harold shouted as he stood up to look out of the window. "The way the judge ruled in favor of the press completely torpedoed my case. She decided that the press isn't liable for fraudcasting all those nasty lies about me to boost their ratings and circulation."

Kimberly leaned back in her chair. "Harold, I'm on your side. But yelling at me isn't going to get us anywhere. Come and sit down."

"I'm sorry, counselor," replied Harold as he took his seat. "My temper got the better of me."

"No problem. But you must understand that you're up against far more than just the First Amendment to the Constitution. You're also up against the right to free speech guaranteed under *California* state law."

"Oh, right. But I thought they were one and the same."

"True…but there are subtle differences. The State of California was the first state in the nation to adopt an Anti-SLAPP statute to protect the right to free speech. This law doesn't exist on the Federal level—only under some state laws. California's Anti-SLAPP statute was designed to stem the flood of libel lawsuits that began popping up after people first used the Internet. This statute is a formidable obstacle to anyone filing a libel lawsuit here in California because the California legislature is determined to safeguard the right to free speech and freedom of the press, even when people post vicious garbage on social media."

Harold Brewster looked down at the floor and whispered, "It's hopeless, isn't it?"

"Well, not exactly. But take it from me, you are facing a serious uphill battle."

"Any chance that I might win *something*?" he pleaded.

"Judge Chang went out on a limb when she applied the Neutral Reportage defense in granting our wonderful mainstream press its motion to dismiss. You may be able to appeal her ruling on the grounds that the judge was making new law for this jurisdiction.

"But please don't get your hopes up," added Kimberly putting up both hands with palms facing Harold. "In my experience, judges seldom change their minds unless they get hammered by the Court of Appeal or the Supreme Court. The judge can—and probably will—find other grounds to support her original decision."

Harold pondered the lawyer's advice. "I understand."

"Filing an appeal at this stage might keep this lawsuit alive long enough for you to discover the identities of those toxic anonymous posters who wrote the nasty posts on Sleuths Anonymous. I'm especially interested in discovering the identity of the individual calling himself or herself Swamp Adder. Excuse the pun, but it seems to me this person wrote the most poisonous allegations against you."

Harold nodded his head several times. "Swamp Adder is the worst of the scumbags. However, the lawyer for Sleuths Anonymous has filed a motion to oppose our request for information about these posters."

"Ah … yes," Kimberly replied with a smile. "I've read Sleuths Anonymous' lawyer, Jack Murphy's motion to quash your subpoena. A recent Court of Appeal decision may prove very helpful in opposing this motion. Swamp Adder wrote several libelous *facts* about you. This may persuade the court to deny the motion to quash. If Sleuths Anonymous is required to disclose any and all information it has about Swamp Adder, we may be able to eventually discover Swamp Adder's identity … or just enough information to track him or her down."

"Well that's sort of good news, isn't it?"

"Maybe. However, I must caution you that even if you win your lawsuit against any of these social media posters, I'm willing to bet that they're 'judgment proof.' Do you know what that means?"

"Sorry, no."

" 'Judgment proof' means even if you jump through all the legal hoops to win a final judgment in court against one or more of these anonymous posters, you learn that they have *zero assets* to pay any legal judgment entered against them, making them what lawyers call 'judgment proof.'"

Kimberly sat back and folded her arms. "Harold, if Swamp Adder turns out to be judgment proof, you and Diedre will have the enormous pleasure of framing the court judgment in your favor and hanging it on your wall because that's all it will be good for."

Harold laughed for the first time.

"That's OK. I'm not in this for the money. I just want to clear our names. I look forward to hanging a judgment on our wall, even if I don't collect a dime."

Kimberly smiled.

"Harold, as long as you understand the potential risks, I am willing to fight on your behalf to the best of my ability. However, you must understand that it's not going to be an easy fight. We probably stand less than a 50% chance of winning anything." Kimberly paused. "It's also important for you to understand that if you lose this case, it won't be because you were wrong in seeking to defend your reputation. If you lose, it will be because the law of libel pitches the right to free speech hard against the right not to be libeled, making lawsuits like yours really tough to win."

Harold again looked down at his feet. "I understand," he whispered.

He rose and Kimberly accompanied him to the lobby.

"Thank you for agreeing to take my case," Harold said, shaking his new lawyer's hand. "It means a lot."

CHAPTER 21

Love Prevails

"Deidre, the news from work isn't good," Harold said as he put his computer on the table and slumped down onto the living room sofa. "In fact, it's lousy."

He looked up as Deidre came into the living room from the kitchen.

"My VC firm doesn't want me to meet with any of its portfolio companies anymore. Apparently, the negative publicity about the libel lawsuit makes me too toxic to be useful. Instead, I'm to stick to desk work…like reviewing FDA approval documents. Frankly, I feel like quitting. But I wanted to talk with you first."

Deidre stared at her fiancée. "Harold, that's rather sudden, isn't it?"

"You bet. Behind the scenes I've learned that the VC partners hate my libel lawsuit. They think I've seriously messed up by filing it… that I've destroyed the cozy relationship with the tech press which I've built up over the years. Now the tech press only writes about the libel lawsuit."

"How did the meeting go with the female lawyer?"

"Better than I expected. Kimberly Hayward didn't talk down to me like that pompous prick Bertrand Wainwright. She went out of her way to say that she's on our side. However, she leveled with me about the chances of winning a reversal of the judge's order dismissing the press: it's probably zero." Harold sighed deeply.

"And that's not all. She also warned me that I face a serious uphill battle getting any information out of Sleuths Anonymous. She doesn't think it's completely hopeless, but she's warned me that my chances of winning anything is less than 50%. I wish for your sake that I'd never gotten involved with this damn lawsuit."

"Harold! Don't say that," Deidre stood behind the sofa and put her arms around his shoulders. "I'm proud of you. Let's get a glass of wine and chat. I've bought a nice roasted chicken from the San Carlos Farmers' Market and some lovely vegetables. It won't take two seconds to put dinner together."

After pouring two glasses of wine, Deidre sat down beside Harold. She covered his hand with her own as they sat side by side.

"Harold, I've watched how hard you've fought for your integrity and reputation against overwhelming odds. You mustn't listen to those idiot VCs who don't understand what it feels like to be falsely accused of committing several crimes. You've fought with courage to set the record straight. I admire that."

Harold tasted his wine and looked at the glass. "Wow, this is nice. Where did you get it?"

"From Roberts Market in Woodside. Given their wealthy and demanding clientele, they have a great wine selection. It's easy for me to pop by on my way back from San Carlos."

Hearing the word Woodside, Harold groaned.

"The worst part is that we may never be able to afford to live in Woodside as I'd hoped. That Woodside Realtor keeps bugging me with new listings. She's wasting her time. After I quit my job, lose the lawsuit, fail to clear my name, and wait forever for the insurance company to pay our claim—if it ever does—I won't be able to afford anything in Woodside."

Tired and distracted, he concentrated on the wide-plank oak flooring.

"Deidre, I'm not the man you thought you were marrying."

Deidre was puzzled and concerned. "What are you talking about?"

"I am not the mega-millionaire that you thought you'd be marrying."

Deidre laughed. "I am so *glad* about that!" She smiled broadly.

Harold looked shocked as Deidre bent over to kiss him.

"Harold, I love you for who you once were…the socially inept techie wrapped up in research who really helps people. However, the huge amount of money you made from selling your company has become a barrier between us. You used to respect people for their *ideas*. Now you and your friends don't think someone's smart unless they're uber-rich, worth millions, and live in a glass palace."

"In other words, I've become a real jerk, haven't I?"

Deidre laughed. "Harold, you are not a jerk deep down. But, to be honest, sometimes you act like one, especially around your wealthy techie friends. Along with them, you assume a swagger that's *obnoxious*. Your conversation is so *narrow*. It's all about renovating mansions in Palo Alto, Pacific Heights, Woodside, or Los Altos Hills. You have no idea how boring that conversation gets after a while."

"Well, I won't be talking about renovating any Woodside mansions anytime soon. That's completely off the table. I will probably lose most of my status-conscious friends."

"*Good*. We'll make new friends, who value us for who we are—not how much money we have."

After a long pause Deidre continued.

"Harold, since working at your current VC firm isn't likely to be much fun, maybe you should return to the type of medical research that improves lives. Since you were smart enough to pay off our mortgages, we can keep afloat financially with my teaching salary and the rental income from my San Carlos condo as long as we adopt a more frugal lifestyle."

"That's what scares me. I paid off your mortgage expecting you'd sell your condo, give up teaching and make the big commitment to become my wife full time. But you didn't sell your condo. You're still teaching. Tomorrow morning you could so easily dump me and go back to San Carlos."

A coldness crept into Deidre's eyes. "You don't know me very well, do you?"

"I didn't mean it that way. But we need to face reality. If I give up my job, I won't be earning *anything*. You'd be justified in giving me the heave-ho."

"Harold, I kept the condo because I want to keep on teaching. I'm committed to helping the next generation become the best they can be. I'm not interested in remodeling mansions. Watching you and your rich friends, I became afraid that eventually you might find a schoolteacher insufficiently glamorous or ambitious enough to be your wife."

"God…I've been a blind idiot. I should've realized that you're as committed to teaching as I was committed to my research."

Deidre took a deep breath.

"Why do you think I was so casual about my ring?" She turned to face him. "As everyone knows, I stupidly left it on the wooden ledge in the back of Tim Newman's cellar. I've been kicking myself ever since. But I took off my ring and left it on the ledge because at that moment I felt my ring was defining my identity in the eyes of your rich friends. It became everyone's sole topic of conversation. I began to feel the ring symbolized the wealth that was coming between us. I *kept* my condo as somewhere I could run to…if and when you dumped me."

As tears fell down Deidre's cheeks, Harold took her hands in his and kissed them. He drew her close to him and kissed her tears. Since the ring's disappearance he'd secretly worried that she believed the ugly, salacious rumors about his dishonesty, about him having a secret lover. He'd also secretly wondered whether the beautiful schoolteacher sitting on his sofa had only stayed with him because of his money. For the first time he realized that she loved and believed in him despite the ugly rumors and *despite*—not *because of*—his money. He was amazed and thrilled to learn that whatever happened to his job and lawsuit, he wouldn't lose his lovely fiancée.

"Deidre, I'm so glad we're having this conversation. I'll never "dump" you. I love you more than anything in the world."

"Harold, we need to get back to what's important to *us*, not what's important to others," Deidre took a stand, speaking earnestly. "I want us to return to the time when we first fell in love and leave behind the person you've become around your rich friends. I *hate* that."

"Deidre, I *love* that you hate that. You're so right. During this ordeal I've learned that some of my supposed new friends can be shallow. They pretend to be sympathetic but I feel a 'holding back' in our friendship that wasn't there before."

Harold again focused on the floor.

"I'd hate being a paper pusher for the VC firm. I need to get back to the lab, even if I don't make much money."

Deidre leaned over and hugged Harold. "Listen, Harold: great Silicon Valley companies were launched in a recession, when there's zero money for start-ups. This is *our* recession. This is the perfect time for you to return to medical research—regardless of the money.

"Deidre, you're wonderful. You're so beautiful and smart. I am so grateful to have you in my life."

They kissed like lovers embracing for the first time.

CHAPTER 22

Anonymous Sleuths vs. Harold Brewster

A young lawyer with sandy red hair; handsome, freckled face and blue eyes rose to address the court.

"Your Honor, my name is Jack Murphy and I represent Sleuths Anonymous. Mr. Brewster has served my client with a subpoena demanding that my client disclose the identities of all anonymous posters who wrote unflattering posts about him on its website. Similar to the *Yelp* case, my client is here today to request that this subpoena be quashed so its users maintain their right to free speech under our nation's constitution."

"Understood, counsel. Please proceed."

"The right of anonymous authors to remain anonymous is a fundamental constitutional right recognized at the founding of our nation. Before our US Constitution was ratified, founding fathers James Madison, Alexander Hamilton, and John Jay wrote the Federalist Papers anonymously arguing for the ratification of the US Constitution. The US Supreme Court ruled early on in our nation's history that an author's choice to remain anonymous is an aspect of the freedom of speech protected by the First Amendment. In recent years, the California Court of Appeal has ruled that websites like Sleuths Anonymous must be put on the same footing as other types of speech."

"Counsel, I have a question," the judge spoke directly to Jack Murphy.

"Yes, Your Honor?"

"The court appreciates you bringing our attention to these rulings. However, the court is also mindful that alleging the commission of a crime is an important *exception* to the right of free speech. Some of the anonymous posts referred to in plaintiff's subpoena clearly allege that plaintiff committed one or more crimes. Wouldn't these posts be libel *per se* and therefore an exception to our constitutional right to free speech?"

"Your Honor is correct. Some of the anonymous writings posted on my client's website did suggest that the plaintiff, Mr. Brewster, committed a crime. However, my client contends that these postings are *not libelous*. Pursuant to the Court of Appeal decisions cited in my client's motion papers, these posts about the plaintiff were either mere speculative opinion or rhetorical hyperbole which any reasonable reader wouldn't take seriously."

"Counsel, I have another question," the judge said to Jack Murphy.

"Certainly, Your Honor."

"In determining whether statements on the Internet are libelous, the California Court of Appeal has also held that the trial court should look at the nature of the website platform where the statement was posted when determining whether a reasonable reader would take the statement seriously."

"Agreed, Your Honor."

"In this context, the Court of Appeal noted that users of some websites often play fast and loose with the facts, or express one-sided opinions that are more diatribe or venting than statements of objective fact. Conversely, other websites encourage their users to share *factual* information about companies and products that a reasonable reader might take seriously. How would you categorize the Sleuths Anonymous website in that context?"

"An excellent question, your Honor. Sleuths Anonymous is a website that encourages its users to help solve crimes by allowing them to post theories and engage in lively debate about who might have committed crimes which have been featured prominently in the news. The website specifically encourages its readers to 'get in touch with their inner Sherloch Holmes' by speculating and theorizing about who might have committed these crimes. It's not a platform that any reasonable reader would view as providing *factual* information."

"Thank you, counsel, please proceed."

"It is important to note that the social media posts about plaintiff did not occur in a vacuum. These posts occurred during a lengthy and free flowing debate about who'd stolen the $50 million diamond ring. During this debate, many users speculated that *other* guests or staff attending the Crush party stole this diamond ring. In this context, it is extremely unlikely that any reader could take the posts about plaintiff seriously because they were contradicted by numerous other posts regarding the other attendees.

"We can all understand and sympathize if plaintiff and others found the posts on Sleuths Anonymous rude and offensive. However, the California Court of Appeal has emphasized that rude and offensive opinions are exactly the type of speech that is protected by the First Amendment.

"My client contends that unless the plaintiff can show that the posts stated *facts* that would lead a reasonable reader to believe the plaintiff had committed a crime, plaintiff's subpoena should be quashed on the grounds that the anonymous authors were *all* exercising their rights to express their opinions—however rude or offensive to the plaintiff."

The judge turned to Kimberly Hayward. "We now request counsel for the plaintiff to address the court."

Kimberly Hayward rose to speak. Harold Brewster sat quietly in his chair watching his lawyer.

"Your Honor, counsel for Sleuths Anonymous is correct in stating that the authors of the Federalist Papers wrote anonymously. He is also correct that the US Supreme Court has upheld the right of authors to write anonymously when exercising their right to free speech under the First Amendment. However, your Honor is *also* absolutely correct. *Not all speech is protected by the First Amendment.* No one has the right to libel or slander another under the First Amendment.

"The US Constitution and the First Amendment were created by a new nation which fought and won the right to be free. However, before our nation rose to demand its freedom, the right of the individual *not* to be subjected to tyranny by the state was also established. More than 800 years ago, Magna Carta was signed, which established an important principle of the rule of law. Under Magna Carta, no man—however powerful—is above the law. Not even the King.

"We live in an era when many are fearful that their employment, their privacy, and even the truth itself are being undermined by social media. Your Honor, I cite Magna Carta because it stands for the principle that no technology company, however powerful, is above the rule of law. Plaintiff has the right *as an individual* not to have his reputation destroyed by anonymous libelous statements posted on an Internet platform claiming that plaintiff has committed several crimes."

Attorney George De Rosa, sitting in the back of the courtroom with attorneys Ann Schiller and Deke Little wrote on his legal pad "Bravo! Every trial lawyer dreams of citing Magna Carta. Kimberly's pulled it off."

He handed the legal pad to Ann. She smiled and passed it to Deke. Deke leaned over to give George a thumbs-up signal. Ann took the legal pad and wrote "Magna Carta's relevance is a bit of a stretch. Kimberly's lucky she's not in Federal court." She handed the legal pad back to George.

George wrote again on the legal pad and passed it back to Ann. She read "Ann, welcome to state court. Our judges are kinder because they know they can be kicked off the bench if one of us opposes their reelection."

Unaware that her lawyer friends sat in the back of the courtroom critiquing the courtroom proceedings, Kimberly faced the judge.

"Your Honor, as stated in the plaintiff's motion papers, the anonymous posters Purple-Headed League and Nurse Watson both wrote on Sleuths Anonymous that my client had conspired with his fiancée to commit insurance fraud in connection with the disappearance of their $50 million diamond ring. There is absolutely no evidence before the court that these allegations are true."

Looking down at her notes, she continued. "Yet another anonymous poster, Swamp Adder, stated that Plaintiff had committed fraud in connection with his start-up company's application for Fast Track FDA approval. As the plaintiff states in his motion papers, if someone is seriously suspected of falsifying anything submitted to the FDA, that individual could face a lifetime ban from any involvement in future medical research submitted to the FDA."

Kimberly stood up even straighter and spoke very distinctly. "Your Honor, this particular false accusation has the potential of irrevocably damaging my client's entire career."

"Understood, counsel. Please proceed."

"Plaintiff has submitted several affidavits signed by accountants and other forensic experts that these online social media accusations against the plaintiff are *completely false*. During the acquisition by Mammuthus Pharmaceuticals of plaintiff's start-up company, Mammuthus hired outside consultants to audit of *all* the information submitted to the FDA in support of the plaintiff company's application for Fast Track approval. It also hired outside accountants to audit this company's financials. These outside experts have all signed affidavits that *no fraud took place* as alleged by the poster Swamp Adder.

"Historically, making a false statement that someone has committed a crime is libel *per se*. We members of the legal profession use the term 'libel *per se*' because it means that the statement is so intrinsically harmful that a plaintiff doesn't have to prove how the statement harmed him. Since the accusations against him on Sleuths Anonymous are libel *per se*, plaintiff doesn't have to show how he might have been damaged by these statements. Instead, the very nature of a libel *per se* statement allows the court to infer that plaintiff's reputation has been damaged."

"Plaintiff respectfully submits that he has presented the court with sufficient evidence that the posts by Purple-Headed League, Nurse

Watson, and Swamp Adder on Sleuths Anonymous were all completely false. Since plaintiff has shown that he is likely to prevail on his libel lawsuit against these anonymous posters, he is entitled to obtain information from Sleuths Anonymous about the identity of those anonymous posters."

The judge put her hand up to signal that she had a question. "Counsel, what about the Sleuths Anonymous argument that the posts about plaintiff on Sleuths Anonymous weren't libelous because (1) they were mere speculative opinion or rhetorical hyperbole which a reasonable reader wouldn't take seriously or (2) the nature of the Sleuths Anonymous website suggests to a reasonable reader that none of these posts should be taken seriously?"

"Your Honor, unlike the other anonymous posts suggesting that others at the Crush party had stolen the ring, the anonymous posts about plaintiff accused him of stealing the ring and committing *other* specific crimes.

"First, Purple-Headed League and Nurse Watson accused plaintiff of both stealing the ring *and* submitting a fraudulent insurance claim.

"Second, Swamp Adder accused the plaintiff of stealing the ring, faking his company's financial statements, *and* faking lab work and animal testing to obtain Fast Track FDA approval. Swamp Adder added that *he had personal knowledge* that plaintiff had a new love interest, suggesting that plaintiff was cheating on his fiancée. These false accusations–piled one on top of the other on the same platform–could easily convince the reasonable reader that the accusations against plaintiff of criminal conduct and fraud should be taken seriously."

Kimberly paused to allow the judge to ask more questions. When the judge seemed satisfied by her argument, Kimberly closed her file.

CHAPTER 23

The Lawyers Share Their Thoughts

Deke, Ann, and George waited outside the courtroom for Jack and Kimberly to exit. Jack walked swiftly past them lip synching "Hello," signaling he was delighted to see them but had to dash off. He signaled to Ann that he would call her later.

A few minutes later, Kimberly followed Jack. She was talking avidly with her client Harold Brewster. When she saw the three lawyers, she laughed. "My goodness, what are you lawyers doing here?"

Ann walked up and gave Kimberly a hug. "I thought you might like some moral support."

"Thanks, my friend." Kimberly turned to George and Deke with one raised eyebrow. "And what's your excuse, guys?"

"As Ann knows, I always support the defense in libel lawsuits," replied George, always the loquacious lawyer. "However, those anonymous social media posts were absolutely vile about everyone, including my longtime dear friend, Amanda Jones, so I have mixed feelings. After we all fought on the same side a few years ago, Deke and I were curious how you and Jack would battle it out in court."

Kimberly smiled broadly. "Fair enough. George and Deke, let me introduce you to my client, Harold Brewster."

After the group shook hands, Harold turned to Deke Little. "Mr. Little, at Deidre's suggestion, I've been reading up about the importance of freedom of the press. I have to say, sir, that I now realize it was probably a mistake to sue your client and other members of the mainstream press."

The lawyers looked surprised. Harold continued. "The social media posts were hideous but I've come to realize that the press was maybe just doing its job."

"So ... you're not going to file an appeal?" Deke asked with a smirk.

"Don't answer that," Kimberly replied sharply to her client. She turned to face Deke. "Counsel, my client did not have the benefit of my advice at the time you and others representing the mainstream press won that extraordinary dismissal of this case on behalf of your clients. Had I been representing Mr. Brewster, things may have worked out *very* differently. Now if you excuse us, we have to be going," she added with a confident smile at her client.

Ann, George, and Deke waited for Kimberly and Harold to walk out of earshot before bursting out laughing.

"Kimberly never gives an inch, does she?" George said.

"Not even a tenth of an inch," Ann replied proudly. "That's why I recruited her to join our defense team in the insider trading case. So, what did you both think of this morning's hearing?"

"Jack's argument was very persuasive but I give the nod to Kimberly," George replied.

"George, you're biased because of those posts attacking my Aunt Amanda. Deke, what did you think?"

"The law is still developing in this area. However, the anonymous posters probably have the upper hand under the current state of the law. Kimberly's argument was magnificent...but my money is on Jack winning this motion."

"Talking of Kimberly, is she correct that things might have turned out differently had she represented Harold Brewster during your client's Anti-SLAPP motion?" Ann asked.

"Who knows?" Deke replied. "However, I will make one observation after attending this morning's proceedings. Harold Brewster isn't the complete jerk that I thought he was."

George and Ann nodded in agreement. "The anonymous posts about Harold were very nasty," George added. "I may be a lifelong member of the ACLU but my sympathies lie with unmasking the people who wrote those nasty posts."

Kimberly walked with her client to her car. After they got inside and closed the doors, Harold apologized to Kimberly. "I'm sorry that I blurted out that nonsense to Mr. Little. I feel like an idiot after you had advised that we might want to appeal the Judge's ruling to buy more time."

Kimberly smiled. "It was a little impetuous, to be sure. But no harm done. Hopefully, the appeal won't be necessary. I'd much rather focus our energies on unmasking the anonymous posters who will make far less sympathetic defendants in front of a jury."

"Do you really think that things would have turned out differently if you'd been my lawyer when the press brought their motions to dismiss my case?"

Kimberly stopped the car engine. She leaned back to ponder her client's question.

"Actually, yes," she replied. "I think things would have turned out very differently. But that's because Deke Little and the other press lawyers wouldn't have brought the Anti-SLAPP motions for us to fight."

Harold Brewster was astonished. "Why?"

She turned toward her client. "I'd have convinced you *not* to sue the press. But we won't let on to Mr. Little and the other lawyers about that, shall we?" She added with a smile as she restarted the car.

Harold laughed "Right on, counsel. Right on!"

CHAPTER 24

The Judge's Ruling

A few days later, an anchorman turned to the camera. Once again, BREAKING NEWS appeared across the bottom of TV screens.

"We have an important news update coming from the San Francisco Superior Court. We are expecting the court to release a ruling regarding whether Harold Brewster will be able to unmask the identities of anonymous posters in the libel lawsuit brought by Mr. Brewster. Our reporter is on the scene at the courthouse in San Francisco. Jennifer, what can you tell us about the latest developments in this case?"

A slim attractive woman holding a TV microphone—now familiar to viewers—appeared on screen standing in front of the San Francisco Courthouse.

"Gerry, last week, attorney Jack Murphy argued before Judge Chang that the website Sleuths Anonymous should *not* be required to provide any information to plaintiff Harold Brewster regarding the identities of three anonymous posters who wrote derogatory, possibly libelous, comments about the plaintiff on its platform. Attorney Jack Murphy argued that the identities of these anonymous posters are fully protected from disclosure under the First Amendment.

"Kimberly Hayward, representing the plaintiff, cited Magna Carta—a famous historical document signed by King John in England in 1215—to argue that powerful technology companies like Sleuths Anonymous should not be above the rule of law. She also argued that three anonymous posters had *per se* libeled her client, Harold Brewster, and that these statements are not protected under the First Amendment and existing case law."

"Jennifer, while we wait for the judge's ruling to be announced, can you remind our viewers what this libel case is all about?"

"A diamond ring worth $50 million given by plaintiff Harold Brewster to his fiancée, Deidre Langton was stolen from the Sonoma home of famed Silicon Valley entrepreneur Tim Newman during a Crush party in October of last year.

"Three anonymous posters calling themselves Purple Headed League, Nurse Watson, and Swamp Adder posted on Sleuths Anonymous that Harold Brewster stole the $50 million ring either because he was in cahoots with his fiancée or to give it to a new secret love interest. I am now getting word about the judge's ruling from my colleague who's reading the decision inside the courthouse." She glanced down at her device and then looked up at the camera.

"Gerry, the judge has ruled that Sleuths Anonymous *does not* have to disclose information in its possession about the anonymous poster, Purple-Headed League, because this poster's comments were mere speculation or opinion and therefore not libelous."

"Wow! Does that mean that anyone can post wild and crazy opinions without this being libel?"

"That's seems to be the court's ruling regarding this anonymous poster, Gerry." She looked again at her handheld. "The court cited California Court of Appeal decisions that mere opinion and/or speculation alone, however rude or offensive, is not libelous under California Law *unless* the opinion is supported by facts that would lead the reasonable reader to think that plaintiff had in fact stolen the $50 million diamond ring."

"That's very interesting. What does the court ruling say about the other posters?"

"The judge's ruling noted that the post by Nurse Watson included facts by stating that plaintiff's fiancée, Deidre Langton refused Lucy Newman's offer to put the ring in the Newman's safe for safekeeping. Instead, Ms. Langton placed the ring on a wooden ledge beside some wine barrels.

However, the court cited other California Court of Appeal decisions that facts cannot support a claim for libel if the facts are *true*. Therefore, the court ruled that Sleuths Anonymous *does not* have to disclose information in its possession about the identity of Nurse Watson."

"This legal analysis is getting complicated."

"No kidding!"

"Anything further?"

"Yes, and this is where it gets interesting. According to my colleague inside the courthouse, the judge also noted that Swamp Adder cited several facts supporting his opinion that Harold Brewster stole the $50 million diamond ring. However, the court noted that the plaintiff has provided the court with sworn affidavits showing that these facts were *false*. The court therefore found that these false facts could lead the reasonable reader to believe that plaintiff had stolen the $50 million diamond ring."

"So, Jennifer, where do these findings lead us?"

"The court concluded that plaintiff Harold Brewster is likely to prevail in his libel lawsuit against the anonymous poster Swamp Adder because these statements are libel *per se*. The court also noted that Swamp Adder failed to state facts in a fair and unbiased manner, which distinguishes these statements from press reports cited in the judge's earlier Anti-SLAPP ruling.

"Bottom Line, Judge Chang has ruled that Sleuth Anonymous must relinquish to plaintiff all of the information it has in its possession regarding the identity of the poster using the pseudonym Swamp Adder."

CHAPTER 25

Swamp Adder's Identity

Kimberly met Harold Brewster in her office foyer and escorted him to the conference room. After she helped Harold to a cup of coffee, she thanked him for coming to her office.

"Harold, I have some good and bad news, which I wanted to discuss with you in person.

"The good news is that Sleuths Anonymous decided not to appeal Judge Chang's ruling about Swamp Adder. Instead, Sleuths Anonymous handed over all its records on Swamp Adder. According to these records, the name of the person using the Swamp Adder pseudonym is John Baker and his address is 221 B Lytton Avenue, Palo Alto.

"Sounds good. What's the bad news?"

"When my private investigator Frank Raleigh went to serve the summons and complaint, he found that the address 221 Lytton Avenue, Apt. B, Palo Alto doesn't exist. It's completely bogus."

"Are you serious?"

"Frank found a large office building on the north side of Lytton Avenue, which takes up the entire 200 Block. This large office building contains several businesses including a bank and stock brokerage. However, there's no 221 Lytton Avenue. Instead, the office building numbering starts with 245 Lytton Avenue.

"Inside 245 Lytton Avenue all the office suites use suite *numbers*, such as Suite 125, 150, 200, etc. None of them use letters, such as Suite A, B, or C.

"On the same side of the street, other businesses occupy premises at 251 Lytton Avenue, 255 Lytton Avenue, or 265 Lytton Avenue. On the opposite side of the street, there's another large office building at 250 Lytton Avenue and a parking lot. That's it.

"That's *all?*"

"No. Frank knocked on all the doors of these businesses to see if anyone by the name of John Baker worked there. He also visited the neighborhood on nights and weekends to knock on the doors of the residential homes in the area. Unfortunately, he came up blank. No one in the neighborhood has ever heard of Mr. John Baker."

"Wow, that's disappointing."

"Yes, I agree. It's a setback."

Kimberly sat back in her chair. "Harold, I'm a fan of the fictional detective stories featuring Sherlock Holmes and his sidekick Dr. Watson. As every Sherlock Holmes fan knows, Holmes lived at 221B Baker Street, London. Unfortunately, it appears that Swamp Adder cleverly concealed his or her true identity by using a Palo Alto version of this famous address.

"My investigator and I discussed whether we'd approach Google to find out if Swamp Adder used the same fictional address for the gmail account. However, we've decided against this strategy. If Google takes down Swamp Adder's gmail, Swamp Adder will just pick another fake name and open another gmail account, which won't advance this investigation one iota."

Harold shrugged. "Ah well. I guess I won't be making any money on this case. You did warn me it might happen."

After a long pause Harold looked at his lawyer and smiled.

"As you know, I set out to prove in court that those nasty posts on Sleuths Anonymous *were* garbage. The judge's recent ruling was helpful because it stated the posts about me and Deidre were either libel *per se* or shouldn't be taken seriously. If you want us to drop the case, I'm happy to do so. Deidre and I are anxious to put this lawsuit behind us and get on with our lives."

Kimberly smiled. "Harold, not so fast. This case is getting really interesting."

"How so?"

"After speaking with my investigator, I've a hunch that Swamp Adder may not be the typical social media type who uses websites like Sleuths Anonymous solely for online entertainment. This may also mean that Swamp Adder may not be the typical judgment-proof anonymous poster lacking the funds to pay your judgment.

"Why do you think that?"

"Swamp Adder has gone to great lengths to conceal his or her true identity. Some posters might do this out of hand. However, Frank and I have a hunch that the fake address on Lytton Avenue was carefully planned.

"Frank thinks that Swamp Adder must have visited Lytton Avenue to select an address that might look legit online…but on closer inspection turns out to be bogus.

"I've also re-read Swamp Adder's posts. As I said before, Swamp Adder's posts were the most poisonous. However, they also reveal a *personal* animosity towards you that isn't reflected in other Sleuths Anonymous posts. Therefore, it's possible that this poster is particularly obsessed with you. He or she may have a personal motive to damage you by spreading lies and rumors about you and your fiancée.

"Harold…got any idea who this person might be?"

CHAPTER 26

The Avian Network Reports To Sidney

A white heron swooped down to the Palo Alto windowsill where Sidney snoozed inside.

"Hey, Sidney. Wake up."

Sidney opened one eye. He groaned. The white heron persisted.

"You asked for our help in finding Swamp Adder, who wrote all those nasty things about Harold and his company. We've discovered something important. A woman techie was observed weeping in her car. She gets tearful whenever she arrives or leaves her workplace. The nearby squirrels and birds report that this woman's boss is using his management position to hit on her, which is now a big problem in Silicon Valley."

Sidney sat up. *"This guy is hitting her? That's terrible. She should go to the police,* he replied indignantly."

No, silly. He's hitting on her, meaning he's groping her, propositioning her— trying to get her alone for sex. When she rebuffs his advances, he bullies her by making scathing remarks about the quality of her work in front of other team members in their department. Stuff like that."

Sidney was confused." *But why is this relevant to us finding Swamp Adder?"*

"Sidney, for a smart Aussie, you are being remarkably dimwitted today."

Sidney sighed sadly. *"Sorry. I'm upset. I was so pleased when Harold won his battle to unmask Swamp Adder! Unfortunately, this anonymous poster used a fake name and address to log onto Sleuths Anonymous. To make bad news worse, no bird or animal has any information about the wildlife witness who was in the cellar the night the diamond ring disappeared. Nothing seems to be working out."*

"Sidney, stop whining. Let's focus on Swamp Adder. We birds have observed

that when a human is mean to underlings in the workplace, it's often the sign of a narcissistic personality."

"What's a narcissistic personality?"

"Someone who acts in a manner that tells us clever birds that they only care about themselves. They think the rules don't apply to them. They lack empathy for other humans. Since this guy's being mean and selfish to this female employee, he's obviously a narcissistic jerk."

"OK…but there are plenty of narcissistic jerks in Silicon Valley. Why do you think this guy's Swamp Adder?"

"Because this guy used to work for Harold's start-up. That's the connection."

The heron paused for Sidney to absorb the information.

"Apparently, he left Harold's start-up before the acquisition that made several people like Harold super-rich. That might've made Mr. Adder super-jealous."

"Wow!" Sidney stared at the heron.*" Jealousy could be a motive for posting that load of rubbish about Harold and Deidre."*

"True. We birds have been following this jerk and we've recently observed him visiting a nearby library in Palo Alto. A local pigeon reported observing the man typing on a library computer—luckily next to one of the library windows. A pigeon reported that this guy signed in as Swamp Adder. Pigeons often boast that they're smarter than the rest of us birds, so I don't give a lot of credence to this report. However, this jerk's use of a computer in a public library signals that he may be trying to conceal his identity."

"But what can I do about it?" Sidney whimpered with exasperation.

"Listen, Sidney. We birds have consulted among ourselves. We need you to introduce your humans to this jerk's female employee. Once they find out that she's being abused at work by a former employee of Harold's start-up, they may connect the dots."

"How in the heck am I supposed to introduce this woman to Lucy and Tim?"

The heron flapped her wings impatiently. *"Sidney be patient. I haven't finished. By following her car, we birds have also learned that the woman works out at the same gym as your human mum, Lucy."*

Sidney growled. *"Darn! My Mom's stopped going to her gym after she started being harassed by the press."*

"Sidney, stop growling and just listen," the heron admonished. *"We've come up with a plan. This woman usually visits the gym before going to work. When she arrives at the gym, she often sits in her SUV looking miserable, as if she's too depressed to go inside. Our plan is that you find a way to leave your home, run over to the gym, and make eye contact with this woman while she's sitting all alone in the parking lot. Are you up for this?"*

"I'm up for this," Sidney barked as he stood with the proud stance of an Australian Shepherd at a national dog show. *"For Deidre's sake, I'll do anything to help the humans discover Swamp Adder's identity. Deidre's been through a lot...as have my humans, Lucy and Tim. If I run off, Lucy and Tim will immediately organize a search party. Once I find this woman, I'll be able to herd all these humans together."*

"Sidney, that is a great plan," the heron tweeted. *"When the time's right, we'll come by your home and give you a signal."*

CHAPTER 27

Sidney Herds The Humans

"Hurry UP, Sidney," the white heron warbled. *"Traffic is terrible this time in the morning. Humans are rushing to work. Be careful…that idiot nearly ran you over."*

"I'm running as hard as I can," Sidney whimpered.

"You're doing great! Only two more blocks until you reach the gym."

A young woman with short black hair sat in her car feeling numb. After yesterday, she didn't have the energy to go into the gym for her workout. *"I hate myself. I don't have the energy to look for another job. Some days I want to kill myself."*

She took a sip of her water. *What have I done to encourage my boss to keep coming on to me? Why won't he leave me alone when I tell him I'm not interested?"* Tears ran down her cheeks. *"What's wrong with me? Maybe I'm coming down with something. Even the birds sound super noisy this morning."*

She heard a loud bark and looked down. A beautiful red and white sheepdog looked up at her from the street, his blue eyes sympathetic

"Hi, big guy?" Isabella said as she got out of her SUV. "You look lost."

After Isabella left her SUV door open, Sidney jumped into the driver's seat of Isabella's SUV. Isabella smiled at the sheepdog's apparent desire to take charge. She got into the passenger's seat beside the beautiful Australian shepherd. Sidney whinnied at Isabella's water bottle and looked up at her. She understood his plea. She filled her cup and offered it to Sidney. He gulped down the water.

After she gave Sidney more water, she searched for a collar hidden in the long fluffy fur of the neck that framed his handsome face. Once her fingers retrieved his collar, she found Sidney's name tag. She grabbed her cell phone.

"Hi, my name's Isabella Depont. I found a sheepdog outside my gym. I think he's lost. His name's Sidney Newman and this phone number is on his collar. Is he yours?"

Lucy nearly choked with relief. "Hi, I'm Lucy Newman. Yes…he's our missing Aussie. He somehow managed to get out. We've been searching for him everywhere. Where are you?"

"I'm outside the Do-It-Now gym."

"Thank God! I'm also a member of that gym. I'll be right over. Please keep Sidney safe until I arrive."

Sidney smiled at hearing Lucy's voice over the phone. Isabella put down her cell phone and sat beside Sidney stroking his long silky fur. Sidney put a large paw on her arm. He looked lovingly at her face.

Isabella smiled. "Big guy, you're the best thing that's happened to me in ages." She bent over and gave him kiss. "You've made me feel useful for a change."

Sidney returned Isabella's kiss with a lick. "*We love you, Isabella. We animals and birds know all about that bullying boss of yours. I'm here to help.*"

When Lucy arrived in the parking lot, Sidney jumped to the back of the SUV. He stared at Lucy's SUV. After he whimpered, Isabella knew Sidney's human mom had arrived. As Isabella exited her SUV and opened the truck door, Lucy saw Sidney smiling at her. Lucy also recognized Isabella as a member of her spinning class, which she'd abandoned after the theft of the famous jewel.

"Thank God you found our darling Sidney. What's your name? It's silly that I don't know, but I always had to rush off after class to take my daughter Catherine to school."

After Isabella introduced herself, they tried to coax Sidney to jump out of Isabella's SUV, to no avail. Sidney jumped back over the barrier to the back seat and jumped into the front passenger seat. He stubbornly refused to leave the SUV.

Lucy felt mortified. "Isabella, do you mind driving Sidney to my home? I'll lead the way. Sidney must be seriously traumatized...but I need to get him home. I'm so sorry if this interferes with your workout."

Sidney gave Lucy a withering look. *"Mom it's not me who's traumatized... it's Isabella. We need to feed and comfort her. You need to hear her story."*

"Lucy, no problem. Don't worry about my workout. Getting Sidney home safely is far more important."

"Great! I'll fix breakfast for us."

After breakfast, the two women sat at the table in Lucy's kitchen sipping their coffee. Sidney sat next to Isabella, leaning against her. After Tim left to drive Catherine to school, Lucy turned her attention to her guest.

"Isabella, you're going to get tired of hearing this, but I can't thank you enough for saving Sidney. Tell me about yourself."

Glancing away, Isabella sighed. "Lucy, I may have helped save Sidney, but *Sidney also saved me.* I've been having a really lousy time at work. I know I should leave, but I don't have the energy to look for another job. Besides, I really love my work as a computer programmer."

After a long pause, Isabella smiled and stroked Sidney's ear. "This darling dog made me feel that I've finally done something right."

Lucy looked at her new friend's sad, peaked face. "Tell me what's going on. Maybe I can help."

"I don't want to trouble you with my problems. But there is something you should know. My horrible boss is a bully. He keeps hitting on me. When I say no to his advances, he makes me look bad in front of my work group. It never ends."

"God, that's terrible," Lucy replied. "Have you told anyone about this?"

"No because the moment anyone complains about anything at work in Silicon Valley, they get labeled a troublemaker. If I complain, it'll be the end of my career."

Lucy replied by slowly nodding her head in sympathy.

"But he doesn't *just* bully me," Isabella said with anger in her voice. "My boss loves to brag around our department how he's the anonymous poster Swamp Adder who's attacked Harold Brewster on Sleuths Anonymous about the missing $50 million diamond ring."

Lucy stared at Isabella. Her facial expression froze. She was amazed at what she was hearing.

"Jeez, Isabella…Harold Brewster's a close friend of ours. This ring disappeared from our home in Sonoma. Harold and his lawyer have been trying to find out who the heck this Swamp Adder is. I can't believe you know him."

"Yes…but I'm not sure I want to get mixed up in this libel lawsuit."

Lucy took a deep breath. "I completely understand how you feel. No one wants to get mixed up in anything that ends up in court. However, it would be really helpful if you'd talk with someone you can trust about all this. Your SOB boss can't be allowed to get away with this crap."

Isabella looked down at the handsome dog who just put a large paw on her knee.

"I've been wanting to talk to someone about my boss harassing me and how he's Swamp Adder…but I didn't know how to go about it without losing my job." She looked up at Lucy with frightened eyes. "If my boss finds out I've told you that he's Swamp Adder, he'll fire me."

Lucy took another deep breath. "We must find a way to get this info to the right people without your career being damaged."

After a long pause, Lucy stood up. "I know. I'll contact our lawyer, Lillian Johnson. She'll know how to handle this. She's very smart and savvy. Anything you tell her will be totally confidential. Are you comfortable with me calling her?"

"Yes, I'm glad you know a lawyer that might be able to help."

Lucy picked up the phone to call Lillian Johnson as Sidney looks admiringly at both women.

The birds outside the window chirruped loudly. *"Well done, Sidney!"*

CHAPTER 28

Swamp Adder Releases More Venom

"You'd get much better pay and rewards if you were a little nicer to me," the man said as he walked out of the building with a younger woman.

"You mean…if I slept with you?" Isabella replied scornfully, glaring at him.

The man who posted under the pseudonym Swamp Adder smirked.

"Something like that…yes," he said as he leaned over to put his arms around her shoulders.

"Leave me alone and stop harassing me," shouted Isabella, pushing the man away. "Haven't I told you a zillion times that I'm not interested?"

Anger replaced the smirk. "You're making a very big mistake, young lady."

Isabella walked away disgusted. However, instead of tears, her eyes sparkled. She knew that Frank Raleigh, Kimberly Hayward's private investigator, was walking right behind her and her boss as they left the building. As she drove home, she prayed that the investigator overheard their conversation. After she arrived at home, she dialed a number on her cell phone.

"Can I speak with George De Rosa, please?"

After a pause a deep sonorous voice came on the line. "George de Rosa speaking."

"George, it's Isabella. I think you'll be pleased. My boss followed me out of the building tonight after work. As planned, Kimberly's PI was right behind us when my boss pulled his usual crap. The idiot can't stop propositioning me, even when I make it crystal clear that I'm not interested."

"Like the male of the species, he's not thinking with his brain," George replied. "He's thinking with his you-know-what."

Isabella smiled. "It's so great having you as my lawyer. You make me laugh."

After Isabella walked away, Isabella's boss was annoyed. However, he knew how to put himself in a better mood. He got into his car and drove to a nearby public library. He rented one of the library's loaner laptops. Walking over to a table by the window, he smiled at the misery he was causing Harold Brewster.

At lunch, he'd joked with his work buddies how Harold's victory over Sleuths Anonymous hadn't succeeded in unmasking his identity. One of his buddies sneered that it was only a question of time before Brewster's libel case was thrown out of court. After opening the laptop and using the library's free Wi-Fi to log onto Sleuths Anonymous as Swamp Adder, he typed and uploaded a post.

"Harold Brewster and his lawyer Kimberly Hayward must have thought they'd scored a huge victory when they forced Sleuths Anonymous to reveal my identity. WRONG! Obviously, these idiots think we Silicon Bros don't know how to protect our ID.

"I can understand this idiocy from an incompetent female lawyer like Kimberly Hayward. No decent Bay Area law firm would hire her after her former firm, Hampton & Elliot, went bust. Harold Brewster only hired this attorney because Brewster's big firm lawyer, Bertrand Wainwright, withdrew from the case after he wised up about his client's true character. Word's out on tech street: Brewster's about to get fired by his VC firm…and about time!

"Brewster used to be smart…but any Silicon Bro who's stupid enough to buy his fiancée a $50 million engagement ring is obviously losing it.

I guess the zillions he made during the recent sale of his company to Big Pharma addled his brains. Maybe Brewster's worried that Golddigger Deidre wouldn't marry him unless he paid millions for her suspiciously missing engagement ring. He should be worried. No woman would marry that dude unless mega millions were part of the deal.

"*No word from anyone about what happened to the engagement ring that's been missing for more than a year. The police seem stumped, which brings me back to my original theory. It's obvious that Harold Brewster had the most to gain by stealing the ring. Only Brewster and his crooked fiancée can keep the ring and bank the insurance proceeds. They should've been arrested and jailed months ago. Can't understand why the authorities are acting so dumb. Did Brewster bribe someone high up not to bring charges?*"

Unknown to the man using the Swamp Adder pseudonym, Kimberly Hayward's private investigator, Frank Raleigh had followed him to the library. The private investigator sat at a nearby desk reading the latest postings about Sleuths Anonymous on his laptop while he waited for Swamp Adder to finish typing. After Swamp Adder shut the laptop, the private investigator tapped Swamp Adder on the shoulder.

"Mr. Smythe, I have something important for you." The private investigator handed an envelope to the other man. The label on the envelope was addressed to John Smythe with 'Law Offices of Kimberly Hayward' printed on the top.

"What the hell is this?" demanded the other man.

"Have a good evening," replied the private investigator as he returned to his laptop.

After opening the envelope and staring at the deposition subpoena, John Smythe quickly returned the laptop and left the library.

The private investigator smiled as he reread the latest posting by Swamp Adder on Sleuths Anonymous. He made a careful note of the time of the posting. After closing and packing away his laptop, he went to the library kiosk marked *ANSWERS*.

"Hi, my name is Frank Raleigh and I'm a private investigator," he said, showing the librarian his ID. "I'm following up on information about a few Internet posts sent from this and other libraries using the libraries' free Wi-Fi. Pursuant to my client's subpoena, can you provide me copies of the records showing the dates and time that Mr. John Smythe rented one of your laptop computers?"

"Mr. Raleigh, the City Attorney's office informed us that you might be coming by," replied the librarian. "Let me take a look at our records. Ah, yes. One of my colleagues has already copied the requested material. I have the information here," the librarian said as she handed the investigator an envelope.

"Thanks, that's very helpful."

After the private investigator left the library building and returned to his car, he looked carefully at the information in the envelope. He matched the information to social media posts on Sleuths Anonymous. After reviewing the records, he called Kimberly Hayward's cell phone and left a voicemail message:

"Hi Kimberly. It's Frank Raleigh here. You'll love the latest post by Swamp Adder on Sleuths Anonymous. It's so flattering about you personally…I don't think! The good news: by using information provided by Ms. Depont, I was able to follow our friend to the public library that's closest to his workplace. Our hunch was correct. I observed him renting one of the library's laptops. After he started typing…lo and behold… a new post by Swamp Adder suddenly appeared. After he logged off, I served him with your deposition subpoena.

"I also picked up the library records we requested from the City. These show that our friend had rented a laptop at this library on the exact date and time of all the other Swamp Adder posts on Sleuths Anonymous.

"Given these records and the information from our friend's coworker, we now have conclusive evidence linking Mr. Smythe to Swamp Adder."

CHAPTER 29

Josh Kaplan Gets Involved

"Hi, Josh, long time no see," Ann Schiller said, seeing her former US Attorney's office colleague, Josh Kaplan.

"Wow! Ann, it's great to see you too," replied the tall handsome federal prosecutor, Josh Kaplan. "I expect you're visiting your Aunt Amanda. I'm also visiting my aunt and uncle here in Sonoma."

"I hope your visit is happier than mine. My Aunt Amanda is still upset by those nonsense social media posts that allege she stole that $50 million ring. These posts seem to have finally died down. Even so, Sonoma is a small town that rumbles with rumors, so those posts still annoy her. This investigation is dragging on, which is taking its toll. Any word, Josh, as to who stole that darn diamond ring and what's happened to it?"

Josh smiled. "Even if I knew the answer, I couldn't share it with you, Ann. However, I understand your concern. If one of my relatives were caught up in this mess, I'd be concerned, too."

"Josh…you're a nice guy, even if we had our differences in the past over that insider trading case. Yep, it's really stressful for the guests at the Crush party. I just wish someone would find the thief, so that everyone else can resume their normal lives."

As Josh walked away from Ann, he pondered the problem of the missing diamond ring. He'd also read press reports about the wild rumors and speculation on social media. As a legal expert on the presumption of innocence, he was concerned about the toxic impact of these wild rumors on the people mentioned in the posts.

After being raised in Sonoma, Josh was also concerned that the unsolved mystery of the missing ring hung heavily over the community.

Residents and visitors must wonder if their valuables were safe. The local Sonoma sheriff's department had been severely criticized for failing to discover any clues leading to the arrest of the thief.

The following morning, while driving back to San Francisco, Josh decided to take a more active role in the case. He pondered the time when he suspected several guests at the Crush party of being involved in an illegal insider trading conspiracy ring. At that time, everyone working in Silicon Valley had been desperate to save their companies or their venture capital portfolios during the Great Recession. Now that the tech economy was booming, the theory that the same techies or their friends stole a $50 million diamond ring seemed ludicrous to Josh.

"Even if one of the techies succumbed to greed, it isn't their type of crime," he thought to himself. *"Massaging the books to meet quarterly projections…yes, they all do it. Embellishing the attributes of their tech or biotech products? Right on the money. Stealing an easily recognizable diamond ring to sell to a wealthy collector…not so much. Selling the ring through shady underworld connections… extremely unlikely."*

Back at his office, Josh decided to discuss the case with Nate Hastings, the prosecutor overseeing the criminal investigation into the diamond ring's disappearance.

"Hi Nate, do you have a minute?

"Sure, Josh. Take a seat," the jovial lawyer motioned for Josh to sit down.

"Yesterday, I was in Sonoma visiting my aunt and uncle. I ran into a former colleague of ours, Ann Schindler. Ann's now a partner with Horace & Fitzgerald. Unfortunately for Ann, her Aunt Amanda attended the infamous event in Sonoma where the $50 million diamond ring disappeared. Ann tried to pump me for information about how your criminal investigation is coming along."

Both lawyers smiled knowingly at one another.

"Obviously I told her that I couldn't divulge any information.

However, as you know, I'm originally from Sonoma. I prosecuted several Sonoma residents for insider trading a few years ago. I thought I'd check in with you on how things are coming along with the investigation of this infamous diamond ring."

The jovial lawyer's smile disappeared. "Josh, during the last twelve months, our agents and local police have been working long hours to uncover anything that might lead to an arrest. Unfortunately, I have to tell you that we know damn all about what happened to that ring. We haven't uncovered any clues. We haven't identified any suspects … except the names and addresses of all the people who were in the wine cellar that night. They've been extensively interviewed and they've all been extremely cooperative. Nothing's been revealed that brings us any closer to discovering what happened."

Josh was stunned. His colleague continued. "Our agents have been carefully monitoring all the bank accounts of the hosts, guests, and the staff for evidence that someone privately sold the ring to a wealthy collector. Nothing so far. Our FBI techies are keeping an eye on the dark web for any hint of a sale or exchange of bitcoin that might resemble the value involved here. Nothing so far. Our international allies are carefully monitoring the high-end jewelry trade. They haven't come up with anything.

"Various local, state, and international investigative agencies have put subtle pressure on the usual suspects who buy and sell valuables on the black market. They've also kept a careful eye on banking activity in well-known money laundering jurisdictions. They haven't come up with anything either."

Nate sat back in his chair. "Josh, our agents have a sixth sense. They've concluded that someone at the Sonoma event stole the ring…*and kept it.* However, that doesn't make sense, either. All the suspects are either famous socialites, high-level techies, or local Sonomans. Why is god's name would they risk being found guilty and sentenced to a lengthy prison term by stealing a $50 million diamond ring–only to hold onto the darn thing?"

Knowing the cast of characters better than the lawyer sitting opposite, Josh nodded his head in agreement.

"Josh, in the words of our intrepid boss, Jane Phelps, I'm this office's expert on prosecuting the theft of high end art, jewelry, and other valuable collectables. However, you've just reminded me that you're our hometown boy with local contacts in Sonoma.

"After your insider trading case, you must know the Silicon Valley and Sonoma suspects better than anyone else in this office. Since we now suspect that this diamond ring is still in the hands of someone who attended the Crush in Sonoma, it might be helpful if you kept your ear to the ground when you're next in Sonoma. I'd like you to find out who the locals suspect did this."

Josh smiled back at the older lawyer. "Good timing. I already have plans to spend Thanksgiving with my aunt and uncle. I'll try to pump them for the latest gossip. I'll also contact Ann Schiller. Ann's very anxious that this investigation be resolved quickly for the sake of her aunt. She may prove a useful ally."

As Josh got up to leave, he added. "Nate, it's a long shot but—Sonoma being Sonoma—I am willing to bet that someone in Sonoma knows something."

CHAPTER 30

The Sonoma Avian Network Investigates

The winged creature descended noiselessly in the dead of night. Professor Owl's intelligent, round flat face peered into Woodrow's ancestral home. Woodrow, known to his family and friends as Woody, knew nothing of the owl's close proximity. He was too busy gloating over his treasure which sparkled in the moonlight while others in Woodrow's household slept peacefully.

"Woody you've been super smart and super dumb at the same time," Professor Owl thought to himself. *"Officer Hawk will be very interested in what I've observed tonight."*

Minutes later, Professor Owl found the large, red-shouldered hawk sleeping. The owl woke the hawk. *"Officer Hawk, I have news about the whereabouts of the diamond ring and the identity of the thief."*

The hawk stared at the owl. *"Does the thief still have possession of the ring?"*

"Yes…and it's still in Sonoma. However, the thief escaped detection by your excellent Avian Highway Patrol because he is clever and devious. He only brings the ring out at night when most humans, animals, and birds are asleep."

"How did the thief make off with the ring?"

"I can only guess but the thief must have followed its owner and observed where the ring was hidden. When Crush of the grapes began, the thief nabbed the ring and made off with it before anyone noticed it was missing."

"Hmmm—smart thief."

"Ah ha…caught you!" screeched Officer Hawk staring at Woodrow, who was still admiring Deidre's diamond ring. *"The humans guessed right. You are an obsessive collector."*

The tiny dusky-footed woodrat looked around anxiously. He saw two large predators, Officer Hawk and Professor Owl staring at him through the branches and twigs of his family's wood nest.

"This ring belongs to me and you can't take it away," Woodrow replied, trying to sound brave. *"I picked it up after the humans discarded it in a nearby cellar. We dusky-footed woodrats are eco. We recycle those items the humans throw away."*

"Oh really?" Officer Hawk could barely control his frustration. *"Since when did any human discard a diamond ring worth $50 million? Woody, be reasonable! This isn't an empty Coke bottle or shiny DVD that you retrieved from a human's recycling bin. You're responsible for putting the Avian Highway Patrol and the human police force through a lot of trouble. Now, give it up immediately."*

"Shan't…and you can't make me," Woody sneered. *"You say that the humans didn't discard this ring. I say different. When humans want something kept safe, they put it in a safe — not on a wooden ledge on the wall behind some wine barrels."*

"Give me the ring or you're likely to face some very unpleasant consequences," Officer Hawk replied sharply. *"Once it's discovered that you've stolen the ring, I hate to think what the humans will do to you and your entire family."*

"How will they find out?" the thief countered.

"Sidney Newman, a smart domestic sheepdog with a highly sensitive nose lives in the home where the ring disappeared. His humans are very upset that the ring's disappeared because they and all their friends are suspected of being the thief. Sidney's asked for our help in locating the wild creature who was in the cellar the night the ring disappeared. Sidney thought this creature might've witnessed one of the humans stealing the ring. Obviously, this so-called witness is you, Woody. Once I tell Sidney that you're the thief, he'll herd the humans to this spot. They'll soon tear your nest apart to find the ring."

"What's going on?" Mrs. Woodrow, who'd arrived from another part of the wood nest demanded. *"What's all this racket? I have my little ones back here and we're all trying to sleep."*

The hawk peered into the nest to address the squeaky voice. *"Hi, Mrs. Woody. Your brilliant husband has stolen a very precious ring belonging to the humans. Once the humans discover that the valuable ring is here, they'll arrive and make a lot of trouble for you and your family. Despite my words of caution, your husband refuses to give up the ring so that it can be returned to the humans…no questions asked."*

"Woody, we have to give the ring back," said the thief's wife to her husband. *"I love that you found it and brought it home as a gift. However, it isn't very useful. It doesn't bring much moonlight into our home or add useful flooring, like our other sparkly valuables."*

"I'm not afraid of those humans," Woody squeaked, ignoring his wife.*" Let them do their worst."*

Officer Hawk looked severely at both dusky-footed woodrats.

"As I said in my lecture to the Sonoma Wildlife Council, humans are very careless with the lives of us wildlife. We kill for survival…but the humans often kill us with their cars and trucks when they drive too fast along our country roads without paying attention to the wildlife around them. We members of the AHP constantly patrol Highways 121 and 37. It's pitiful the roadkill that we see along these highways."

As Officer Hawk paused. Professor Owl chimed in. *"Officer Hawk is correct. I see roadkill all the time among our community. It's very sad to see the animals and birds killed for no reason."*

Officer Hawk puffed out his chest. *"When the humans discover the missing diamond ring is in your home, they'll take it out on you. They'll take your ancestral home and other similar nests apart until they confirm that you haven't sneaked off with any other valuables. I know this because I've seen my human counterparts be very tough if they suspect the laws have been broken. Sometimes they pull people over on the road and haul them off to spend the night in jail. If you're smart and know what's good for you, you will allow me to return this ring."*

Mrs. Woody became increasingly alarmed as the Hawk and Owl spoke. Finally, she'd had enough.

"Woody, I can't have my great grandmother's ancestral home destroyed overnight because you've walked off with something valuable belonging to the humans. We must give this ring to Officer Hawk. He knows best."

"No human is allowed to disturb our habitat because we're a Species of Special Concern, which gives us special rights," replied Woody with a stubborn look in his eyes. *"We're not like the common Rattus Norvegicus rat that lives in dirty places and spreads disease. We dusky-footed woodrats are clean and fastidious. We're known as 'nature's architects' because we build elaborate wood nests lined with bay leaves to keep out fleas and other pests. We're also known to be 'nature's innkeepers' because our nests provide clean habitat for other species."*

Woody stood up indignantly. *"Officer Hawk, you talk to me as if I'm a common thief because I added this ring to my collection. I am not a common thief. I added this ring to my collection because it had been discarded at the back of a cellar. I have a respectable reputation to uphold as a sophisticated collector with discriminating taste. I demand compensation for this ring before I'll part with it."*

CHAPTER 31

The Avian Network's Advice To Sidney

"Sidney, the Avian Network has asked me to tell you the good news," tweeted the white heron. *"Officer Hawk has found the thief and the ring."*

Sidney stared at the white heron. *Wow…that's great!*

"Officer Hawk needs your help ASAP to get the ring away from the thief and returned to its rightful owner. You must return to Sonoma ASAP."

Sidney sighed. *"You members of the Avian Network are keeping me busy. I want nothing more than to help Officer Hawk get the ring back to Deidre. But here's the problem. Lucy and Tim aren't planning to go up to Sonoma until Thanksgiving weekend. I don't know how to persuade them to go sooner."*

"Hmm," the white heron said thoughtfully. *"Sidney, let's try to communicate with Catherine. Child humans like Catherine are closer to nature than adult humans. They're more sensitive to animals and birds Maybe we can signal to her that your family's presence in Sonoma is needed urgently."*

Sidney and the white heron went in search of Catherine. They found her on the patio with a coloring book and new crayons. Sidney went over to sit beside her. He placed a large front paw on her lap. The white heron left to round up other local birds.

"Hi, Sidney," Catherine smiled down at the large dog. "OK…I forgive you for running off the other day. However, you were a naughty dog. We were all *very* worried about you. Sheepdogs aren't supposed to run off. Labradors and golden retrievers often run off to explore their neighborhoods. Sheepdogs are supposed to stay with their herd. Dad says that since you don't have any sheep, your herd is *us*. You need to stay and protect us."

Sidney looked at the child with love in his eyes. *I know. You're so right…*

but I had to save Isabella.

Catherine stroked the dog's ear. "My new aunt Isabella is wonderful. We are so lucky she saved you."

Sidney's smile changed to a pout. *"I saved Isabella. The adult humans gave you incorrect information."* Sidney's smile returned. *"But that's not your fault."*

"Whenever Aunt Isabella and Mom work out at the gym together, they bring me lovely doughnuts," Catherine continued enthusiastically. "The other night Dad told Mom that his VC friend Marc Todd wants to hire Aunt Isabella for one of his startups. Mom replied that this was good news, but Aunt Isabella wants to stay put until Harold's lawyers get enough evidence to punish her nasty boss."

She leaned down to whisper in Sidney's ear. "Mom and Dad don't know that I know this. I sometimes sit on the top of the stairs at night listening to them talk after I've been put to bed. I know a lot more than they think I know," she giggled.

"Me to." Sidney smiled broadly at the child.

"I'm smarter than they think."

"That makes two of us," Sidney panted.

After the white heron rounded up the local birds, they began tweeting loudly from nearby bushes and trees.

"Sidney, do you hear our birds calling to us? They must be hungry."

Catherine went to check her bird feeders. Sidney accompanied her.

"The white heron's correct," Sidney thought. *"Catherine's much smarter than the adult humans when it comes to listening to birds."*

"Sidney, now I'm worried about our birds in Sonoma. I need to check our bird feeders there, too. Sidney...come!" She ordered the large dog. "We have to go inside and find Mom. I need to tell her that we need to check our bird feeders in Sonoma ASAP. The weather is getting cold up there. We have to feed our birds before they all starve!"

The birds flapped their wings in delight. They flew into nearby trees and bushes to report the latest news to the squirrels and other wildlife.

CHAPTER 32

Sidney Herds Law Enforcement

On the Saturday after Thanksgiving, attorneys Josh Kaplan, Ann Schiller, and Lillian Johnson sat with Lucy Newman in the Newman's living room in Sonoma. Lillian Johnson asked Josh to begin the discussion since he'd requested the meeting.

"Thank you, counsel. Since I've been spending Thanksgiving with my aunt and uncle here in Sonoma, one of my colleagues working on the diamond ring investigation asked me to contact you and Mrs. Newman to ask if I could view the area where the ring disappeared. My colleague also wanted me to ask you whether you'd heard any local gossip that might help our investigation."

"God…I wish I *had* heard some local gossip," Lucy replied sadly. After a long pause she added, "forgive me, everyone, for being distracted but I'm really worried about our sheepdog, Sidney."

"What's the problem?" asked Ann.

"In Palo Alto, Sidney escaped and was lost for several hours. After he was rescued by a lovely woman called Isabella Depont, our daughter Catherine became very concerned about her bird feeders in Sonoma. She constantly pestered Tim and I to return to Sonoma earlier than we'd planned. After we arrived in Sonoma, we caught Sidney overturning our recycling bins and picking up shiny soda cans and other shiny objects in his mouth.

"Yesterday Catherine told us that she'd spotted Sidney rushing towards the creek with a soda can in his teeth. Catherine has a very lively imagination. She imagines that the birds in Palo Alto begged her to check her Sonoma bird feeders. Therefore, we shouldn't take Catherine *too* seriously."

Everyone nodded and smiled at Lucy.

"However, Sidney overturning the recycling bins is so unlike him. He normally never goes near them. We're worried that he's coming down with some canine illness."

Hearing his name, Sidney gave a loud howl from a nearby room. "*Let me out. Let me out,*" Sidney barked. "*I have information that will help with the investigation.*"

"I shut him away so that he wouldn't jump on you," Lucy said as the group heard the sheepdog's howls and barks.

"Oh, please let him out," Josh replied with a broad smile. "I *love* Aussies. They're very smart dogs."

After Lucy let Sidney out of his crate, the huge sheepdog flew in the air as he bounded into the room. Seeing a longtime friend, he galloped over to Lillian.

"The rodeo's arrived," joked Lillian as the sheepdog's front paws landed on her lap. "Lucy, Sidney doesn't look sick to me."

The sheepdog jumped off Lillian's lap and stared at the two other lawyers, Ann and Josh. He ran over to the French windows. He instantly returned, stared at the three lawyers a second time, yelped and galloped back to the French windows.

"He's done this before," said Ann. "It means he wants us to follow him outside."

"No kidding," said Lillian. "These sheepdogs are very expressive, aren't they?"

"Also quite bossy," said Josh with a smile. "Let's see what he wants."

"I expect he just wants to go walkies, but we'll see," Lucy replied.

After Lucy opened French windows, the sheepdog ran to the back of the property by the wine cellar. The group followed. By racing several yards ahead and returning to herd the group, Sidney eventually led them along the creek. The sheepdog suddenly stopped and looked down at the creek bank whimpering.

"Look over there," Ann said, looking in the direction of the sheepdog's stare.

On the riverbank beside the creek, a shiny object glittered in the sunlight.

"Wait here while I investigate," said Josh. He slowly climbed down the river bank and made his way to the shiny object, followed closely by Sidney. He removed his cell phone from his pocket and dialed Ann's number.

"Ann…I'm calling you on my cell because I don't want to shout," Josh whispered. "But I think I've found the missing $50 million diamond ring. I'm going to call the Sonoma Sheriff's department and ask them to get someone over right away with a CSI kit. Maybe Lucy and Lillian can meet them at the Newman's house and bring them to this spot. You and I should stay behind to make sure nothing happens to this ring."

As they waited for the local police to arrive, Josh looked around and noticed several tall willow trees in the area. One willow tree caught his attention. A large mound of twigs resembling a wooden cone was propped up against the tree.

"Ann … I have a hunch about the identity of our thief, "Josh whispered on his cell. "See that pile of twigs over there in the shape of a cone? It's a wild dusky-footed woodrat's nest."

After Ann gasped in horror, Josh said "Don't be alarmed. These creatures aren't like ordinary rats. They're almost golden-colored, tiny little creatures, who resemble gerbils. They live quietly in wooded areas like this close to creeks. They're famous for stealing shiny objects, like soda cans, DVD's, shiny ballpoint pens…you name it."

Josh moved closer to the willow tree to carefully inspect the twigs. "Ann…I can see a couple of shiny soda cans in the nest. However, I mustn't get too close because these nests mustn't be disturbed. I'll try to take some photos."

After Josh took several photos of the nest and the ring, he stood back admiring the tall nest. "Ann, ever heard of the expression 'pack rat' to describe people who don't throw anything away? The expression comes from this tiny creature who lives in the same nest for generations and collects mountains of stuff."

After the local Sonoma Sherriff's department arrived, Josh scrambled up the river bank. Sidney stayed behind to guard the ring.

"Hey, Josh, great to see you man," Deputy Dan Carter said as he got out of the police cruiser.

Josh Kaplan shook the police officer's hand. "Let me introduce you to my former colleague, Ann Schiller."

With the introductions made, Josh Kaplan pointed to the river bank. "We think we've found the missing $50 million diamond ring. However, before we touch anything, we wanted to notify your department so that you could carefully remove it for analysis."

Josh Kaplan and the police officer scrambled down the side of the riverbank and over to the dog guarding the sparkly object on the river bank. "Hey, big guy," the police officer greeted Sidney holding out his hand to show he had excellent dog manners. "You're the Newsman's Aussie. We've met before, haven't we?"

"*Yes, I never forget a scent,*" Sidney replied with a smile and a lick of the deputy's hand."

"Sidney's one smart Aussie," Josh Kaplan replied. "I don't know why he lead us here. But he insisted that we go for a walk along this creek. After we arrived at this spot, we found the ring."

The police officer stared at the ring.

"Wow…I was at the Newman residence shortly after the valuable engagement ring disappeared. This certainly fits the ring's description. But how the hell did it get here? Who would leave such a valuable diamond ring on a river bank this way? This is nuts!"

"Hopefully the lab analysis will reveal some clues," replied Josh quietly.

"However, I have my own suspicions."

"Fire away," the police officer whispered looking up at Lucy Newman suspiciously.

"See that dusky-footed woodrat nest over there," Josh pointed to Woody and Mrs. Woody's home. "My hunch is that our culprit lives in that wood nest or a similar nest close by."

"You've got to be kidding me!"

"Nope," Josh replied. "I'm serious. If I'm right, none of us will be making an arrest anytime soon. Wildlife thieves are outside our jurisdiction," he joked.

The police officer stared at the nest and at the ring. "Well I'll be damned! As a kid, I learned that those tiny creatures love to collect shiny objects." He chuckled.

"Wait until I tell the folks in our department that one of these creatures is the devious thief who stole the $50 million diamond ring. They'll laugh their heads off."

CHAPTER 33

The Press Conference

Harold and Deidre followed Kimberly Hayward to a desk placed on a podium facing members of the local, national, and international press. Attorneys Ann Schiller, George De Rosa, and Deke Little sat at the back of the large hotel conference room unobserved.

Kimberly was the first to speak into the microphone.

"We are delighted at the recent news reports that the Sonoma Sheriff's Department with the assistance of US Assistant Attorney Josh Kaplan retrieved Deidre Langton's engagement ring. The ring was discovered lying on a riverbank by the creek that runs at the back of the Newman property in Sonoma.

"At the request of the local police, researchers at a Bay Area naturalist research center detected small traces of rodent saliva in the crevices of the Violette Diamond, consistent with the saliva of a dusky-footed woodrat. The authorities have confirmed that the forensic lab, which carefully analyzed this ring, found rodent saliva, bay leaf, and tiny rodent teeth marks around the ring's shaft.

"Naturalist experts have confirmed that small dusky-footed woodrats often collect and hoard bright shiny objects, such as soda cans and DVDs. However, to date no dusky-footed woodrat has been known to have stolen a diamond ring worth $50 million. That's a new one for the books. Fortunately, the large La Violette diamond and the smaller white diamonds weren't damaged.

"Most importantly, no human fingerprints were detected on this ring. Therefore, Lucy and Tim Newman and all the staff and guests present when this diamond ring disappeared have been exonerated from any involvement in this ring's disappearance."

Kimberly turned towards Harold and Deidre. "My client Harold Brewster and his fiancée are delighted to announce that they will no longer be proceeding with their insurance claim. Mr. Brewster has a few comments before we open this up for questions."

Harold look bashful as he took the microphone from Kimberly.

"Deidre and I always knew we were innocent of stealing our own ring. I filed my libel lawsuit to prove that simple truth. I wanted to prove in court that the social media posts about me and Deidre were unfounded lies and mean-spirited speculation. I think I accomplished that. However, I now believe that my lawsuit against members of the mainstream press which reported what was happening on social media was a big mistake."

The room went completely silent.

"Unintentionally, my lawsuit against the press did not exonerate me as I'd hoped. Instead it made me look an arrogant bully. I stand before you today as a humbled man who has learned to appreciate the importance of the press in protecting our constitutional right to free speech.

"I have also learned an important lesson watching my darling Deidre conduct herself with dignity and grace throughout the police investigation. From the time her engagement ring vanished, Deidre refused to suspect anyone of theft. She was always convinced that the truth would eventually come out and that we and most of our friends would be exonerated. Blessedly, she was right."

Harold returned the microphone to Kimberly.

"Any questions?" She asked the press.

One reporter's hand shot up. "I would like to ask Ms. Deidre Langton why she's not wearing her $50 million engagement ring." The room erupted in laughter.

Deidre smiled broadly as she took the microphone from Kimberly. "We've decided to sell my engagement ring." The room again went silent. After a long pause she continued.

"I met and fell in love with Harold before he became wealthy and famous. We've decided that we need to return to an earlier time in our lives before Harold found himself in the media spotlight. Being famous is really not our style. After living through the loss of this fabulous diamond ring, the police investigation, the social media lies and distortions, and the libel lawsuit setbacks, we've decided to take time off to chill and just be together. Selling this ring will give us the funds to allow that to happen."

"What do you both plan to do after you've taken time off?" another reporter asked.

"Harold wants to return to the lab to discover new products and therapies to help people suffering from incurable illness and disease. I'll continue to pursue my passion, which is teaching the next generation."

"I have a couple of questions for Harold Brewster," a reporter shouted. "Why do you think Mr. Smythe attacked you personally on Sleuths Anonymous? What's the status of your libel lawsuit against him?"

Deidre passed the microphone to Harold.

"I will leave the legal question to my attorney," Harold replied with a smile. "However, since everyone has had such an entertaining time speculating as to the identity of the thief who stole our valuable diamond ring, I will speculate on perhaps some the motives behind the social media attacks against me, Deidre, and our friends.

"Some people log on to social media for online entertainment. I think that many people reading and writing posts on platforms such as Sleuths Anonymous fit that category. Unfortunately, in today's world, too often the nastiest, most vicious posts get the most attention. To be noticed, some people resort to attacking others to win what they believe is their fair share of attention.

"I have also observed that some people think success is a zero-sum game. They wrongly believe that for them to be successful, others must fail. Clearly, this might be true if one is pursuing a career in sports, where only one person or team can win. However, this isn't true in Silicon

Valley. It's not the Silicon Valley way. Here in Silicon Valley there's always room for everyone to succeed. I will now hand the microphone to my attorney to answer your second question."

"Thank you, Harold," Kimberly replied. "As a lawyer, I try not to speculate. I only deal with facts. The fact is that we successfully discovered the identity of the person using the pseudonym, Swamp Adder. We have learned that Mr. Smythe was at one time an employee of Harold's start-up. He left sometime before the start-up was sold to Mammuthus Pharmaceutical. With this in mind, I must emphasize that this individual's accusations of criminal conduct by my client were completely false. However, it is not my job to speculate as to the motives of his attacks on social media.

"In wrapping up this conference today, I wish to emphasize that my client's libel lawsuit against this individual is ongoing. Thank you."

After Harold and Deidre left and the press had filed out of the room, Kimberly joined her lawyer friends, Ann, Deke and George.

"I think it's time for a celebratory drink, don't you?" she said smiling.

CHAPTER 34

Swamp Adder's Secret Weapon

A young lawyer with angry eyes walked into the lobby of Kimberly Hayward's law office. "My name is Clarissa Neville and I have come for an 11:00 meeting with attorney Kimberly Hayward," she said belligerently to the receptionist.

"Please take a seat and I'll let her know you're here," the receptionist said quietly. He was secretly amused by the hostile demeanor of the young lawyer. "God save us from those young lawyers who think they must always act tough," he thought to himself.

Kimberly Hayward arrived and showed Clarissa Neville into the conference room by the lobby, Kimberly looked at the cheaply printed business card. She recognized the address as a virtual office used by San Francisco lawyers to avoid the expense of maintaining a fulltime Financial District presence.

"Congratulations on starting your own practice so soon after being admitted to the California Bar," Kimberly said with a smile, offering Clarissa a cup of coffee.

"Not exactly my first choice," Clarissa replied bitterly. "You might as well know…I couldn't get a job after law school. I decided to hang out my shingle after the Bar results came out."

Kimberly decided to cut to the chase. "What would you like us to discuss?"

"My client, John Smythe asked me to meet with you. He's recently lost his job because of company's been embarrassed by his behavior. He's also going through a nasty divorce. I'm here to tell you that you can't get blood from a stone."

"True, but my client suffered great anguish over what your client wrote. He deserves some recompense."

"If your client suffered over the trash written about him on social media, he's a fool. No one with any brains takes social media seriously. It's a form of entertainment – like the movies and reality TV. That's why recent California Courts of Appeal decisions has made it super tough for anyone, including your client, to bring a lawsuit for libel."

She paused. Kimberly remained silent. She was secretly a little impressed by the young lawyer.

"If your client also suffered over what's been written about him in the so-called mainstream press, he only has himself to blame. Your client has admitted in front of the cameras that suing the press was a really dumb move on his part."

Clarissa paused to take a sip of coffee. Kimberly remined silent.

"If your client's reputation took a beating, it wasn't because of what my client posted on social media. It was because members of the press turned against your client after he sued them. The puff pieces about your client being everyone's favorite biotech entrepreneur ceased. They were replaced by hostile pieces about his libel lawsuit."

"I thought we were meeting to discuss your client...not mine," Kimberly replied.

"My client's been incredibly stupid as well," acknowledged Clarissa. "Most of the nerds working in Silicon Valley can be super smart and dumb simultaneously. Haven't you noticed?"

Kimberly smiled. "Tell me more about your client, so that I can go back to mine with an argument as to why my client should settle this lawsuit."

"As I mentioned earlier, my client's going through a divorce. Divorce does strange things to men's heads, especially those who are socially inept...like Mr. Smythe. They suffer a feeling of worthlessness, which often makes them do really dumb things."

Kimberly felt less smug. "Women suffer in divorce as well," she replied.

"Yes, but most women know how to cope with the little things in life. They also have women friends who help them through the worst of being alone. They don't take success and failure in the workplace quite as seriously as men. Too many men's identities and sense of self-worth is based on how successful they are at work. If they fail at work, they feel they've failed at life."

Kimberly nodded, acknowledging the truth of the young lawyer's argument.

"Your client may not remember, but Harold Brewster and Mr. Smythe were colleagues at Stanford. Seeing your client become so wealthy and successful after my client left his start-up hurt my client deeply. Most people will dismiss Mr. Smythe's behavior as jealousy – and they would be right to do so. But jealousy can consume and destroy people worse than any drug. I know this is no excuse, but your client's success made my client feel inadequate. My client's recent divorce, coming on top of everything else, made him do incredibly stupid things. Mr. Smythe' social media posts using the pseudonym "Swamp Adder" was an example of him acting from jealousy."

As Clarissa talked, Kimberly thought about her own jealous feelings about her husband's new love interest. For the first time, she thought she'd be open to mediating a settlement between Mr. Smythe and her client.

"Are you representing your client in the divorce?" Kimberly asked quietly.

"No, I'm not representing him in the divorce proceeding. I had to draw the line on that. But I am representing him in the sexual harassment matter, which got him fired. I'm disgusted at the way he behaved towards Isabella Depont. I've learned through the grapevine that she's a really nice, smart woman who was forced to work under very difficult circumstances. I'm seriously pissed with Mr. Smythe behaving like a predator toward someone so young and sweet. I've told him that my sympathies lie with the opposition."

Kimberly's eyebrows shot up. This brutal assessment of a client's behavior was a new type of advocacy.

"I've also told my client that I'm also disgusted at his sexist posts about you, one of the most successful female lawyers in San Francisco."

"Oh, goodness," Kimberly replied. "I've been so busy handling Harold's case, I'd forgotten those posts."

"Well I haven't. As a newly minted attorney, it's important to me that all female attorneys be treated with respect, even if we are on opposite sides. I've told Mr. Smythe that he's got to reform – get help. He's got to stop being a jerk around women, including his soon to be ex-wife. Being a jerk around women is no longer cool. It's disgraceful."

"And your client is OK with you expressing your views so candidly?"

The young lawyer smiled sadly.

"Obviously he's not thrilled. But he puts up with it. He's my Dad."

CHAPTER 35

Deidre And Harold's Wedding Reception

Several months later, everyone was in a party mood at Lucy and Tim's home in Sonoma.

"How do you feel about your ring being stolen by a dusky-footed woodrat?" Amanda Jones asked cautiously.

"I'm very grateful that it was a tiny dusky-footed woodrat, and not one of our friends, that stole the ring," replied Deidre looking down at the replacement ring on her left hand. "However, I'll make darn sure that no *other* dusky-footed woodrat steals any of my jewelry in the future."

Both women laughed and hugged.

"It's time for us to taste our latest wine from the barrel," announced Tim. "But first, Harold wants to say a few words."

Harold Brewster moved forward and stood in front of assembled guests. "My friends, I don't know how to thank you all for your kindness and generosity in coming here today," he said. "I need to apologize for initially suspecting anyone of you of stealing Deidre's ring. Fortunately, as I said to the press, Deidre had more sense. She refused to believe that any of you had stolen her ring … and she was right."

The group smiled sympathetically at Harold. They secretly knew that they'd also suspected one or more of their closest friends during the police investigation.

"Please raise your glasses to my darling bride, Deidre."

After everyone enthusiastically clinked glasses and drank Deidre's health, Harold continued.

"I'd also like to thank Ann Schiller and Josh Kaplan for finding Deidre's ring and helping the police discover the truth about its disappearance."

"Hear, hear," went the cheers.

"Thank you everyone," replied Ann. "But it was Josh's knowledge about Sonoma's rich and colorful wildlife which solved the mystery of the ring's disappearance. I'll never forget his lecture about the hording habits of the dusky-footed woodrat after we first spotted the ring." Everyone laughed.

"Ann, I don't think I deserve the credit," replied Josh. "Most of the credit goes to Sidney, our sheepdog sleuth. Like the dog, Toby, in the Sherlock Holmes' mystery *The Sign of Four,* Sidney led us to the whereabouts of the ring. Let's drink to Sidney."

On hearing his name, Sidney got up to be petted and given dog treats.

A child's voice suddenly cut into the celebratory mood. "Mr. Kaplan's *wrong,*" said Catherine defiantly. "Sidney is not a good dog. He's a bad dog for abandoning his family and running off to the creek."

Lucy went over to Catherine, followed closely by Sidney. "He didn't run off, sweetheart," Lucy explained. "Instead, Sidney persuaded us to follow him to the creek where we found Deidre's ring."

The child paused. "Oh, OK. Sidney, I forgive you," she replied stroking the large dog's fur. "Why don't adults explain things properly?"

A green heron and a songbird flew by. "*Well done, Sidney,*" squawked the green heron. "*Woody is bragging to his family and friends how he profited from trading the ring for the shiny objects you brought him. What a scoundrel! Still…it's typical of a woodrat. They love shiny objects. The bigger the better.*"

"*Officer Hawk is proud of you,*" sang the songbird.

"*Thanks for all your help,*" replied Sidney with a big smile on his face.

After the humans broke into smaller groups, Amanda Jones turned to her friends, Lady Roberta and George De Rosa. "Darlings, we must ask Kimberly Hayward to sit with us at dinner. This is the first social occasion she's attended since becoming single. Although she knows a few people here today, she looks rather sad and lonely."

George looked over at Kimberly and nodded at Amanda. He put his arms around his friends. "Be careful, ladies," George whispered. "We can't appear to be patronizing Kimberly. She's as proud as the devil."

Sidney's sharp ears picked up George and Amanda's quiet words. *"When everyone sits down to eat. I'll go sit by Kimberly to comfort her,"* Sidney thought to himself.

Deke Little arrived and also noticed Kimberly standing by herself. He marched over and gave her a big hug. "Great to see you, Kimberly. Let's get a drink," he said with a big smile. He guided her to the bar and picked up two glasses of Gloria Ferrer Blanc De Noir sparkling wine. "Cheers to the new married couple. Nice of you to get the hosts to invite me. I mustn't forget to say hello to them."

"Even though you're a member of the plaintiff's Bar, they'll still be pleased to see you," Kimberly joked. "Seriously, I want to thank you for helping me organize the press conference. Harold and Deidre were very pleased and relieved at the press coverage they received from that meeting."

After they worked the room, Deke motioned Kimberly to sit down for a quiet talk.

"I was really impressed with your argument about the right of the individual at the Sleuths Anonymous motion hearing. Speaking about the rights of the individual…"

"Keep talking." Kimberly said, amused at this compliment from opposing counsel.

"I'm also thinking about the fact that you're now single," he said looking at her sideways.

"You are correct," Kimberly said bitterly. "I'm now on my own. Like almost all deceived spouses, I was the last to know about the new love interest." Kimberly put on a brave smile. "My ignorance must have amused the legal profession in the City."

Deke didn't smile. "No one's amused, Kimberly, at what you've been going through. It could happen to the best of us…and frequently does.

We lawyers work long hours, which puts a huge stress on any marriage. In most people's eyes, it's your ex who looks the damned fool."

Kimberly looked at Deke. "Thank you. I appreciate that."

Deke finally smiled. "When convenient to your schedule, how about lunch or dinner?" He asked in a lighter tone of voice.

Kimberly looked at the deep crevices in the lawyer's face as he smiled. She also saw a sweet sympathy in his eyes. She found the combination irresistible.

Kimberly leant over. "Are you asking me for a date? If so, aren't we on opposite sides in court a little too often? What will our clients think?"

"Ann and Jack seemed to manage OK. Besides I'd never let a client dictate my personal life…such as who I ask for a date. I suspect that you wouldn't either."

"As a member of the GOP, aren't I too politically incorrect for your Democrat friends?"

"I've lost track what's politically correct and what isn't. But after listening to you standing up in court for the rights of the individual, I'd fight to the death for what you believe in."

Kimberly smiled. "Deke. I'd love to have lunch or dinner with you sometime."

George joined his longtime friends, Amanda Jones and Lady Roberta. "I've heard via the grapevine that Kimberly and her husband sold their condo for a huge price. Hopefully that's some consolation for her," George said solemnly looking over at Kimberly.

"Lady Roberta and I were just commenting what a scumbag her ex is," replied Amanda.

"Kimberly could do worse than hitch up with Deke Little," George said, raising his large bushy eyebrows at both women. "Deke has a lovely house in the Marina and a full-time chauffeur who drives him around the City."

"Oh, darling you shouldn't have told us," replied Lady Roberta mockingly. "We'd have thrown our hats at him … wouldn't we, darling?"

She turned to Amanda Jones.

"You lady cougars are far too expensive for Deke," George teased.

A few minutes later, George left Amanda and Lady Roberta to speak with Kimberly and Deke.

"I recently had a settlement conference with Mr. Smythe and his lawyer about my client Isabella Depont's sexual harassment claim," George said quietly. "Smythe's young lawyer, Clarissa Neville is something else. She tore into her client in front of us about his despicable behavior. However, she also made the excellent argument that there's probably no money available for Smythe to pay any judgment. Isabella is now thinking about settling the case with her former employer and foregoing a lawsuit against Smythe in return for a public apology. She just wants to move on."

Kimberly laughed. "Same with Harold's case. Harold just wants to get on with his life."

"No one can blame him for that," George replied.

After the guests took their seats for dinner, Sidney laid down between Catherine and Lucy, as Kimberly didn't need him. He felt exhausted.

"I can't understand why humans pay enormous sums of money for flashy pieces of carbon called diamonds," Sidney sighed to himself. *"Jays are mean-spirited birdbrains and woodrats aren't the brightest...but you'd think humans would be smarter. I wish my human herd would all stay in one place, so that I can keep an eye on them and keep them out of trouble."*

Sidney heard a small creature rustling around in the nearby bushes. He got up to investigate.

"Oh no...not you again!"

"Of course, why not," Woody replied with pride. *"I always turn up for fancy social gatherings in my neighborhood. I've been grooming myself all day. When the humans clean up, I'll recycle as much of the shiny decorations that I can get my paws on. Some of these colorful decorations will look wonderful in my nest. As I told Officer Hawk, I'm very eco-friendly. I don't like to see anything shiny go to waste,"* he added smugly.

Sidney sighed deeply. *"Just stay away from diamond rings. OK?"*

THE END

Acknowledgments

I wish to thank members of the private wine consortium Double Barrel Winery and the owners of the commercial winery David Clinton, who've educated my husband Bill Monnet about wine making. Bill helped me write Chapter 1 based on his personal experience crushing grapes.

I wish to thank Squire Patton & Boggs partner, Joseph Meckes, who shared his experience counseling clients about libel law, Debra Beresini who described the role of an entrepreneur-in-residence at a venture capital firm, FDA expert Michelle Yelmene, who provided valuable information about the FDA's Fast Track approval process, and crime authors and attorneys George Fong and Vilaska Nguyen who gave me invaluable advice at the 2018 Book Passage Mystery Writers Conference about how the authorities would investigate the loss of a $50 million diamond ring.

I wish to thank Marin Open Space Trust, the Nathanson Stewards of Nathanson Creek in Sonoma, Open Space Sausalito, the Sonoma Ecology Center and Wildcare in Marin who educate all of us how to cherish and protect our wonderful Bay Area wildlife. Information provided by these organizations helped me developed Sidney's colorful wildlife friends.

I wish to thank my writing support group members Linda Pfeifer, Lisa Dearborn and Jennifer Berry who provided valuable input while I wrote this novel.

Once again I received expert advice from my editor Deb Carlen, my book cover designer Patti Britton, and my book layout artist Todd Towner.

Finally, I'd like to thank my family and friends who have patiently waited to read this novel.

The wait is over.

CPSIA information can be obtained
at www.ICGtesting.com
Printed in the USA
FSHW021701061019
62722FS